Also by Chandler Morrison

*Hate to Feel*

# JUST TO SEE HELL

CHANDLER MORRISON

Just to See Hell

By Chandler Morrison

Copyright © 2015 by Chandler Morrison

All rights reserved. No part of this publication may be reproduced, distributed, or transmitted in any form or by any means, including photocopying, recording, or other electronic or mechanical methods, without the prior written permission of the publisher, except in the case of brief quotations embodied in critical reviews and certain other noncommercial uses permitted by copyright law.

This is a work of fiction. Names, characters, businesses, places, events and incidents are either the products of the author's imagination or used in a fictitious manner. Any resemblance to actual persons, living or dead, or actual events is purely coincidental.

ISBN-13: 978-1515297604

ISBN-10: 1515297608

Cover art by Lauren Rynee

For S & M
Shine on, you crazy diamonds.

# **Contents**

Satisfaction    3

April Showers    25

Pleasant Times Away from Home    49

To the Face    61

Sick Again    73

Somewhere Between Screaming and Crying    89

Objects in Mirror    123

Mechanical Patriots    137

Rocket Man    143

Body and Blood    175

Coming Down    201

*"First you take a drink, then the drink takes a drink, then the drink takes you."*

*---F. Scott Fitzgerald*

*"When we start deceiving ourselves into thinking not that we want something...but that it is a moral imperative that we have it, that is when we join the fashionable madmen."*

*---Joan Didion*

*"The world is better off with some people gone. Our lives are not all interconnected. That theory is crock. Some people truly do not need to be here."*

*---Patrick Bateman*

## **Satisfaction**

Trekking past shelves lined with endless provisions packed to surging excess, the huge fluorescents glaring down like enormous white suns unrelenting in their intensity, shoppers filing by with their tiny little lives condensed into the coldly vacant galaxies within their unblinking black pupils...and all of this is only just beyond the periphery edge of my attention. My awareness is being greedily dominated by the tiny hand tugging at my own, and the little voice piercing through the cacophonous raucous of this horribly ultramodern marketplace, whimpering, "Hurry, Daddy. Daddy, hurry. Hurry, I'm not gonna make it."

His free hand is clutching his crotch, and his customary toddler's toddle is even more stiff and awkward than usual. The small round face is scrunched up in agony, his eyes huge with something that looks like terror.

"Don't hold yourself like that," I say in an even tone barbed with passive annoyance. "It's not going to make any difference, and you're just making yourself look ridiculous."

He either doesn't understand these instructions or just chooses not to acknowledge them, because he only squeezes his groin harder and continues to whine.

*He doesn't need diapers anymore*, she'd insisted to me just two nights ago, lying in bed and smoking her menthol cigarette and drinking her bubbly white wine while I undressed and readied myself for much-needed sleep. *I know most kids his age still wear them, but he's more advanced than them.*

I had looked at her quizzically when she'd made this claim, and I asked her, *Advanced how? In what ways is he advanced?*

She'd just shrugged, downed the rest of her wine and stubbed out her cigarette in the heart-shaped ashtray and then refilled her glass. *In all ways. He's just...advanced.*

And so here we now find ourselves; me hurrying our in-all-ways-advanced son to the grocery store's restroom while the darling Missus scours the cosmetics aisle. I can feel my blood starting to gurgle up to its boiling point, can feel myself slipping to the very place that Bill and Bob keep adamantly telling me to avoid. More whimpering, more tugging, and it takes everything in me not to scream at the kid to shut up, *shut up,* SHUT THE FUCK UP.

Deep breaths, turn a corner, follow the arrows cheerily pointing the way to the RESTROOMS. Hanging from the ceiling between two of the burning white suns is a gigantic papier-mâché bird of a species that would be indiscriminate if not for the well-known name of the grocery store chain and the huge sign hanging from its gnarled claws that exclaims, "THANKS FOR SHOPPING AT BIG PIGEON, WHERE YOU'LL ONLY SPEND A SMIDGEN!!!" Some ingenious corporate asshole's latest brilliant advertising pitch, no doubt, and my already-dwindling faith in Commercial America drops another few points.

I've managed to all-but-completely tune my son out, and I'm now just mechanically maneuvering through the maze of shopping carts and sample stands and junk-food displays, hearing nothing but the steady drone of indistinguishable noises and garbled snippets of unintelligible conversations. I sidestep a mountainous heap of a woman who is shoveling boxes of Twinkies and cellophane-encased cupcakes into her cart with a heavy, sagging slab of flesh that might be considered an arm to those with lower standards for the human race. A young girl, probably about my son's age, is holding a crimson bag of licorice and pleading with her mother, tears streaming down her face, and all I can think is, *I bet she still wears diapers.* A man in a sharp business suit, hair prematurely gray at the temples, bumps carelessly past me while barking into his cell phone as a woman calls angrily after him. Two boys no older than six or seven dart up and down the potato chip aisle with plastic guns in hand, pointing them at each other and shouting things like "Bambambam you're dead, motherfucker!" and "I just shot your guts out, asshole, get down on the ground so I can teabag you!"

As we're passing the water aisle, I stop, much to the sniveling chagrin of my son, who starts doing an obnoxious crotch-holding dance that I ignore, for my attention has been diverted to the sole woman standing in the aisle. She has dark skin and peculiar, foreign-looking clothing, likely hailing from some poverty-stricken shithole far to the east, across leagues of wild ocean and miles of sternly-divided airspace.

It is not her ethnicity that gives me pause, however, but instead the expression upon her decidedly not-yet-American face. Her thin dark lips are parted in breathless awe, her gentle eyes wide with incalculable wonderment, the faint lines on her thirty-something face tied taut with something between perplexity and...horror, perhaps? She's fidgeting, picking at her too-short nails and shifting her inconsiderable weight from one leg to the other every few moments. Her slight frame is suddenly wracked with a shivering tremor that winds up her spine. She keeps moving her gaze up and down the aisle, milk saucer eyes drinking in the innumerable jugs and bottles of shockingly varied sizes. Selecting a single bottle of Aquafina, she turns it over in her brown hands, holds it up to her face, presses it to her cheek. Then, with tentative, frail fingers, she twists off the cap, lifts the bottle to her trembling lips, tilts it back, and takes several long swallows. When she pulls it away, she emits a soft, shuddering moan. It's a sound not unlike the ones my wife makes following her rare, legitimate orgasms that are always in such stark contrast to the artificial ones that she thinks are so convincing.

I want to call out to her, to run to her and tell her the truth that she will not find in American television and billboards and propaganda. I want to tell her to go back, water or no water, back to whatever place from which she came. I want to grab her by the shoulders and shake her, shout in her face that *this place will consume her*, it will make her into one of us and violently wrench out any purpose and worth which now may reside within her. I want to tell her to say to *hell* with all of her glorified, preconceived notions about us, to run away and don't look back, for the love of *gawd* don't look back, because Sam's gaze will turn her to stone the moment she makes eye contact. I want to steer her from the bountiful, prettily-painted delights of consumerism and point to the fat, hideous pigeon hanging from the ceiling. I want to say that...*that* is what we really are; we are bloated, bottom-feeding birds too lazy from our gluttonous engorgement to utilize our borderline-useless capability of flight. We are parasites, winged tapeworms plaguing a doomed society, and I want to warn her away before her appetite starts to set in.

    I want to do all of these things, but I will do none of them, because it is too late for me. Americanism has claimed me wholly and completely, and the American Way is to want and want and want but never really do anything about it. Effort and hard work are as foreign to us as the plentiful water is to this woman. We base our pretensions on the delusion that we *do* work hard, but I bet this woman would scoff at our definition of such. I can see in her face that she has seen *true* labor, slaving away beneath suns hotter and brighter than the ones currently above us, enduring back-breaking conditions all in the name of earning a measly fraction of what we "earn" here in the manifested destiny of the West.

My ruminations are interrupted by the slowly creeping awareness of my son's wails as he pleads with me, weeping now. I grumble at him to get a grip and lead him away, down the final stretch towards the elusive restrooms.

When we reach them, I am Ulysses at the end of his quest, Roland at the top of the Tower...my son is a ring, a terrible ring to be cast into the long-sought fires of that horrible black mountain of fabled lore. I am exalted with elation at the notion of an end to his whining by means of an emptied bladder. For a brief moment I'm terrified that it won't work, having been clutched and squeezed for so long...if such were to end up being the case, the miserable wails would only intensify, and that would be it for me. I can't handle any more, not even the slightest increase in the volume of this child's woeful cries. I don't know what happens when people *snap*, so to speak, but I really don't feel like finding out. Not today, at least. Not here in a fucking grocery store named after the *worst* goddamn bird in the animal kingdom.

We're still standing outside the door to the restroom, neither of us moving, and thus I look down at the boy and say with agitated expectance, "Well? Are you going to go or what?"

"You gotta go with me."

*Advanced in all ways*, she had asserted. What a joke, haha, haha, everyone laughs, the crowd goes *wild* and shouts a screaming demand for an encore.

*He's just…advanced.*

"Are you kidding?" I say, my voice prickly and cold.

He shakes his head furiously back and forth, bending his wobbling knees and squeezing himself so hard that I'm *sure* I won't be getting grandchildren from this kid.

No great loss.

"Fine," I say, letting out a seething sigh through my clenched teeth. "Let's go."

The big gray door is closed, but the handle is unlocked, so I turn it and push and it swings open on shrieking hinges.

Something's wrong with Daddy, he looks funny, he just went all white in his face after he opened the door and now he looks funny. I don't like his face looking like that, it doesn't look normal, I've never seen it like that and it looks like the pictures in my coloring book before I color them in. I wish I had some crayons so I could color Daddy in because I want him to look normal again, not all white like that. I wish I could make everything the color I want it to be. He doesn't like something in the bathroom, there's something in there that's making his face look like that because his face was normal before he opened the door but then he opened it and looked inside and now it's all white and his mouth is open a little like he's about to say something but he doesn't say anything.  He's not holding my hand anymore, his hands are just hanging there like they're dead or something, just hanging still from his arms and not doing anything.  Then I remember I still gotta go potty, and we're just standing here, just standing here not doing anything...Daddy just keeps looking straight ahead and I'm looking up at him and trying not to cry because he gets mad when I cry, he gets all mad and then Mommy gets mad, and Mommy is the worst when she's mad, so I'm scared she'll come and see Daddy all mad because I made him mad, and then she'll get mad that he's mad and then she might hit me like she does sometimes, always with the hand with the shiny ring on it that hurts so bad when it hits me.  I don't want that to happen so I can't cry, but I gotta go potty, and we're just standing here and I'm afraid I'll pee my pants, and then Mommy will hit me even more so I gotta go in there and go potty.  I look in the bathroom to see what's making Daddy's face so white...if I find it and hide it maybe he'll stop being scared, because he looks scared, so if I do something to make him not scared he'll be normal again, and then I can go potty, but I don't know what's making him scared.  Maybe it's the words, the words on the sign that I can't read but I know it's purple, the sign is purple and the letters are yellow and maybe they say something he doesn't like, I wish I could read them and know what they say but the only time I can read is when Molly reads to me so maybe that doesn't even really count because I'm not even looking at the words when she's reading to me but sometimes before she leaves when Mommy is giving her money she says that we read a book together, not that she read a book to me, so maybe it does count but Mommy never really says anything, she just gives her the money and then Molly leaves and I'm always sad when she leaves because I like Molly and Daddy likes Molly too, I can tell by the way he looks at her and talks to her…he doesn't look at Mommy like that or talk to Mommy like that, so I don't think he likes Mommy all that much, but I know he likes Molly.  I think a little just slipped out, I think I feel a little wet down there, so now I'm really scared, and I hold my thing down there really hard, and it hurts a little but I don't want any more to come out, and I tell Daddy come on Daddy I gotta go real bad but he doesn't say anything, he's just staring at the man under the sign, so maybe it's the man that's scaring him, but the man doesn't look so scary to me. He looks real tired though, and he's got a booboo on his arm with some blood coming out and there are some weird spots on his arm that might also be booboos but I don't know.  He's got something around his arm too, it looks like the thing Daddy wears around his neck when he goes to work so I don't know why this man has it on his arm, so maybe that's why Daddy is scared, maybe it's because the man is wearing it wrong and he doesn't know it and also because he has booboos. Everything else is shiny and normal, the sink looks regular and the toilet looks regular and everything looks regular so I don't know what Daddy is scared of and why his face is so white but I say to him Daddy I'm about to go you gotta hurry but he still doesn't move and now I'm scared because I feel even wetter but I can't go in there and do it by myself because Daddy needs to lift me up since I can only pee sitting down because when I tried to do it like Daddy and stand and pee I made a mess and Mommy got real mad and yelled and hit me so now I'm only allowed to go when I'm sitting but I can't unless Daddy helps me up. Oh no, oh no, more wet and crying, crying, I can't stop crying, and I can't stop peeing, and I feel it going all down my leg and I see it on the floor, and I scream because I know I'm gonna get in trouble now so I scream and scream and scream and it just keeps coming and I just keep going.

"IF THE CONDITIONS OF THIS RESTROOM DO NOT MEET YOUR SATISFACTION, PLEASE NOTIFY A MANAGER AND WE'LL GET IT CLEANED UP FOR YOU RIGHT AWAY!"

So reads the sign on the bathroom wall in letters loudly yellow against their bright violet backdrop, a cheerful invitation to "HELP KEEP OUR STORE CLEAN" as prescribed by a smaller sign taped to the lid of the trashcan. I keep looking from one sign to the next and then down, down at the man sitting propped against the wall below the first sign, the man with the cornflower blue tie fastened around his scrawny bicep, the sleeve of his neatly-pressed white collared shirt rolled up a few inches above his elbow and a thin trickle of blood racing down the tracks on his pale, narrow forearm. He's sweating, damp black hair hanging down and partially obscuring one of his glassy, washed-out eyes while the other one stares at me with calm disinterest, and the corners of his chapped lips twitch slightly, offering forth a weak, dopey smile. Legs clad in creaseless beige slacks lay splayed out before him in a sharp V, each one ending in a tasseled black loafer that shines glossy and polished in the fierce light of the overhead bulb. Pinned upon his left breast pocket is a green rectangular badge that reads "TERRY REINER" and below that, "GENERAL MANAGER". The needle lays discarded a few feet away on the sparkling white linoleum, its scarlet-tipped point glinting ominously. Beside it is a dormant walkie-talkie shed from its clip on the man's belt, shrugged away like some totem of shirked responsibility.

Am I seeing all this? Is this real? Somewhere far away my son is sobbing and shouting at me and pulling on my limp hand, but none of it registers. All I can do is look into that slow-burning ember of an eye that is whispering to me, soft whispers like tendrils uttering *"What of it? What of it? What are you going to do about it?"*

Suddenly the abandoned walkie-talkie begins to bleat out a crackling squawk of static, followed by a male voice that says, *"Hey boss, I'm awful sorry to bug you, but Karen's out smoking, Beth is on lunch, and no one knows where Ron is so you're the only manager on duty at the moment."* Terry Reiner makes no attempt to answer; his whispering eye just rolls lazily to gaze in the transceiver's general direction, blinking sleepily.

There's a pause as the man on the other end of the transmission waits for a reply, but when he doesn't get one, he continues and says, *"Well, uh, I got a customer here who's looking for a particular type of lady's deodorant called Red Roses and..."* A woman's voice cuts in faintly from the background, her words fuzzy and indecipherable, and then the man corrects himself with, *"Um, sorry,* Bed *of Roses, not Red Roses. She says she buys it from here all the time but she's not seeing it and, um, I'm not either. I don't even see a spot for it so I don't think we could have sold out of it or anything. Do you know if we've got any in back, or did it get discontinued or something?"*

The manager's uninjured arm begins to move slowly, languidly, and for an absurd moment I think he's about to reach over and grab the walkie-talkie, but instead he procures from the pocket of his pants a pack of Pall Malls, which he thumbs open and lifts to his mouth, pulling a cigarette out with his teeth and then letting the pack fall to the floor. He reaches back into his pocket and digs around before removing his hand, empty as it had been before its entry. His wasted eye rolls back towards me and he says in a low, croaking whisper, "You got a light?"

Maybe it's just reflex caused by years of corporate brainwashing, an ingrained sense of submission to authority that permeates beyond the white walls of my own workplace, but my hand instinctively falls into my pocket and pulls out a Bic the same shade of orange as the pack of cigarettes on the floor. I look down dumbly at the wickedly innocent little device in my palm, surprised by its presence there due to the eleven days it's been since I last used it or anything else of its kind. An until-now-unknown habit, I suppose, of continuing to carry lighters despite the recent cessation of my need to use them.

Its purpose fulfilled in a figurative sense before a literal one, the sight of the lighter causes a brief crackle of light to appear in the junkie manager's hazy eyes, signifying a relief only added to that which he no doubt already feels, sweet orange frosting glazed upon a China-white cake. My sweating palm slickens it, and I feel it may slip from my hand if I do not soon rid myself of it. More so, I am suddenly afraid of it; it is a threat, it is mocking me quietly in a manner I cannot describe nor understand, but I must, *must* cast it away before it can do to me unspeakable things, things it thinks in its awful little metal head, grinning at me with fiery bile creeping at the back of its silver throat. My impending act of minor generosity has now become decidedly selfish, for I want the Reiner fellow to have the lighter far more than he knows that he himself wants it.

    And all at once it is gone from my hand, slipping away with eager ease and arcing through the air in an awkward tumble of juvenile somersaults, its flight feeling more protracted than surely it must really be, and then it lands in the manager's narrow lap to be scooped up and flicked, flicked, flicked until upon the third strike the anxious yellow tongue of quivering flame leaps up and gently caresses the end of the cigarette…I can hear that delicious little crackle as paper gives way to ash and ember and I watch with bated breath as pale cheeks sink slightly inward and I can almost *feel* the smoke galloping into his lungs and lingering before being released slowly again into the stale air, curling into cloudy blue plumes around his head. "Thanks," he whispers, barely audible…he is already nodding away, falling into a gray trance neither here nor there nor anywhere, retreating into the vast dark recesses of himself and leaving me out here with a sobbing, shrieking child with soaked pants. Whatever connection previously unrealized we may have shared vanishes, a strained cord snipped at the center by a huge pair of kitchen shears stained greenish-red from the insides of proverbial lambs dragged squealing from the warm comforting tits of their mothers, carried out of barns once thought safe and hauled into slaughterhouses abuzz with the whirring sound of grinding saws. His eyes swing shut like doors slammed in the faces of Bible-wielding carolers and Witnesses and messengers of gawd. I cannot sing. I have no Bible. I do not eat meat.

    I step back. Our business here is done, the junkie having been appeased and my advanced son having already emptied his advanced bladder, never mind that it wasn't where it should have been emptied and that reeking golden puddle is *huge*. I consider locking the door as I pull it closed but think better of it; protecting this man from further discovery is a courtesy I either cannot or will not grant…the extent of my trained submission to authority figures only reaches so far.

    The door clicks resoundingly shut and reality more or less reappears around me, its sudden sharpening of clarity like the reaffirmation of normal pressure and sound following high-altitude ear-popping. My son's shrill cries are more penetrating than ever, and the buzzing drone of dozens of meaningless conversations is overwhelming nigh to the point of being maddening. From invisible speakers somewhere above, Mick Jagger croons about his inability to get "no satisfaction", which is a double negative and thereby he should be *plenty* satisfied so I don't know what the fuck he's whining about, anyway.

    *…IF THE CONDITIONS OF THIS RESTROOM…*

    "I *know* you didn't," I say through gritted teeth at my son, who between sobs is announcing to everyone that he "didn't make it, didn't make it, didn't make it." He's leaving a trail of yellow droplets behind him, and I am all at once filled with shame and embarrassment despite the fact that no one is looking, no one is paying attention, no one seems to have even noticed.

Is any of this happening? Am I happening? Is he? Did the abhorrent bathroom encounter happen? Has *anything* happened?

I feel disconnected, out of touch, like I've stumbled through one of those fabled holes in time-space and I don't know where to go so all I can really do is wait for the men on the chessboard to get up and tell me.

My head is beginning to hurt. My hands are shaking. Blackness is creeping in from the corners of my vision and

*...DO NOT MEET YOUR SATISFACTION...*

my palms are sweating so I lose grip of my son's hand and

*...PLEASE NOTIFY A MANAGER...*

someone else is crying, someone else, someone not my son, and I look in the direction of the cries and find my vision pointed down the long smoking barrel of the water aisle, where the foreign woman still remains, but she is now on her knees and weeping, weeping, weeping and muttering something I can't understand, something that isn't English but is so much more beautiful, like wind chimes in a cool, rainy breeze…and yet there is tragedy in those unknown words, tragedy beyond comprehension, and I look from her to my son and then back to her and think, *That there,* that *is suffering,* that *is something worth crying about.* My son has wet his pants, and right now he knows no tribulation more intense than that. This little incident is the end of the world to him, but I can hear something in that woman's voice and in her strained sobs, something that renders not only my son's accident but *my whole family's entire lives completely irrelevant.* That woman knows misery unlike anything I or my son or my wife will *ever* even *begin* to comprehend.

"GOD BLESS AMERICA" reads the bumper sticker on our minivan.

I am nauseated.

Hand clutching stomach churning with disgust, I force myself to walk forward, force myself not to think of the woman in the water aisle, force myself not to think about the man

*he can't be a man because he doesn't smoke the same cigarettes as me*

in the bathroom, not listening to the boy at my side, just thinking, *one step at a time, don't think, don't think, don't think, just hang on, hang on, this too shall pass, your problems are miniscule and they will pass just as they all do.*

Blindly I stumble through the crowd and suddenly I am there and she stands before me, brimming shopping cart beside her, a stick of Teen Spirit antiperspirant in a delicate hand decorated with long lacquer fingernails, and her makeup-saturated face is pulled down in a frowning grimace wrought with frustration and annoyance.

"They don't have it," she says, her eyes still scanning the aisle as if her preferred deodorant may suddenly appear in a miraculous act of supernatural kindness bestowed unto her by an otherwise-uncaring universe. "For years I've always gotten the same deodorant, and now all of a sudden they don't have it. And the kid who works here couldn't even find a goddamn manager. If I had the time, I'd write a complaint letter, or something. I want to know just what kind of show is being run here."

I look at the stick of Teen Spirit in her hand and the only thing I can think to say is, "I didn't even think they made that anymore."

She looks at it and then tosses it bitterly into the overflowing cart. "Yeah, well, apparently they do. I wore Teen Spirit all through high school so that's what I'm going to get. I just can't believe they don't have *my* deodorant. I just can't believe it."

"You're not a teen anymore."

She narrows her eyes at me, and then her gaze shifts to our son, who has stopped crying but his breath is still hitching and he's wiping great green globs of snot from beneath his nose.

"He didn't make it to the bathroom?" my wife asks, her

face darkening, the fury beginning to fill up the eyes that I fell in love with in days seeming long past, long dead.

"No," I say, my voice deadpan, and I realize with revulsion that I can smell it. The nausea is returning. "No, he didn't make it."

She sighs through gritted teeth and says to our advanced son, "I'll deal with you when we get home. Pull it together and stop drawing attention to us."

The boy nods, but more tears are beginning to stream down his red face and I fear another episode of sobbing is imminent. I'm not going to be able to deal with that. I'm going to need to get the fuck out of here before I lose it, if I haven't already lost it, have I already lost it? I'm thinking of cigarettes that I'm not going to smoke, of all the things I've sworn I won't do but that seem so goddamn enticing at the moment, and then my eyes fall to something in the shopping cart. My wife's gaze follows, and then we lock eyes and she says, "Don't fucking judge me. Just because you're all enlightened now doesn't mean I have to get up on your high horse with you. Don't you fucking judge me."

I'm not judging her, I'm really not. I'm just trying to think of something to say. For years I've always had something to say, always fighting to have the last word, but now I just can't think of anything.

* * *

Something's wrong with Daddy again.  He sees something else he doesn't like, but now it's in Mommy's cart and that makes me scared.  I don't know why Mommy would have anything that Daddy doesn't like but she's mad and he's mad and they're mad at each other and they're mad at me and just mad mad mad and I'm so scared and I'm trying not to cry but I feel it coming, just like the pee, all of these things coming and I can't stop them and it makes me mad just like them and it also makes me scared.  Mommy is saying something to Daddy about horses and she's saying the words I can't say because if I say them she squirts soap in my mouth and makes me swish it around in my mouth and I don't like doing that at all.  They're looking at each other all mean and I think they're about to start yelling just like they always do at home and sometimes outside in other places like the store but not as much but then Daddy takes the jingly keys out of his pocket and they go jingle jingle jingle and he holds them forward to Mommy but Mommy doesn't take them, she just looks at them all mad and says what do you want me to do with those and Daddy says take them and when she doesn't he just drops them in the cart and then turns away and starts walking and I try to follow him but Mommy yells at me real loud and says to come back here, where do you think you're going, and maybe she's talking to him or me or both of us but I stay put just in case, but Daddy keeps going and

I don't know what's happening but it seems bad. Mommy yells at Daddy and says you can't just walk away from me, where are you gonna go, and Daddy keeps walking and says I'm going home and Mommy says how are you gonna get there dumbass, and then Daddy stops and turns around and says real quiet I'm going to walk, I've been walking for some time now, you should try it sometime, you're just standing still, you're just running to stand still. Then he walks away and Mommy is just standing there and I'm just standing here and we're both just standing.

## **April Showers**

So much grime.

All of the self-contrived problems of the "sick", all their whining complaints and pitiful lamentations, their bleating pleas for a pill-shaped panacea to a chronic condition that can be diagnosed only as *life*, and whose prognosis is always nothing less than certain *death*…all of this grime, all of it and more, sliding from April's body and swirling around the shower drain before being mercifully sucked down into the abyssal sewers beneath the shrieking pit of retarded children that is the World of Man.

The steaming water pelts her with its forceful urgency, bursting forth from the shining chromium nozzle like revitalizing rainfall upon a barren desert wrought with drought and decay. She is purified once more, or at least as much as is possible at this stage in her rapid descent into the very ailment she claims to treat.

Salty tears mix with the water streaming down her face. From the stereo in her living room comes Framing Hanley's "Built for Sin", just barely audible over the sound of the shower. Her house is empty. If music plays and only Dr. April Diver can hear it, does it still make a sound?

When she is at last cleansed and the water runs cold, she twists the nozzle and for a few long minutes just stands dripping in the tub, shivering in spite of herself, listening to the droplets of moisture plink down onto the porcelain. Everything else is silent; the music has stopped, leading her to believe it was indeed never playing in the first place.

Or that something turned it off.

This all feels eerily familiar. Like *déjà vu*, but worse.

She tries to hear her heartbeat and cannot, and two delicate fingers pressed to her thin, faintly pulsing wrist is her only confirmation of her continued feeble existence. A brief look at the razor on the edge of the tub opens a world of possibilities, but only for a moment, for the thought is as fleeting as the glance itself.

She gets out of the shower and dries herself off.

She can already feel the grime beginning to collect again.

"It's not because of the accident," April says, looking out over the lake. "That's really not the reason at all."

Jake lights a cigarette and waits a long time before he says, "Bullshit."

And April doesn't say anything.

The sky is gray and the water is calm, quiet. The bench is damp from a recent rainfall and they have their bare feet buried in the cool, moist sand. The beach is empty save for the two of them.

Jake says, "If it wasn't for the accident, things would have turned out differently. Between us."

"You don't know that. It was years ago. Anything could have happened between then and now."

Jake shakes his head, slowly but with a firmly-clenched jaw. "It was because of the accident," he says.

Again, April doesn't say anything. She watches a seagull continue to dive into the water, coming up empty every time. For some reason this makes her feel profoundly melancholic.

"I'm going to join the priesthood," Jake says after another period of silence.

April looks at him but he doesn't look back; he just keeps looking out at the water, smoking his cigarette with strange diffidence. "Why would you do *that*?" April asks him.

Now Jake does look at her, and he says, "What else am I supposed to do?"

"Anything. Anything other than that. It's silly. You don't even believe in God."

"No. But I believe in something, I think. I'm going to live in celibacy for the rest of my life, anyway. I might as well do something that requires it."

"Jake..."

"I want you to know I don't blame you, by the way. It's an important part of a relationship. You really can't have one without it."

"Please stop, Jake." April has tears in her eyes, but she can't figure out if it's because of the conversation, or because the seagull is still failing in its attempts to catch a fish. Maybe it's neither.

There's something else she's supposed to say, April knows, but she can't think of what it is or how to say it so they both just sit there.

"I've always thought Lake Erie was ugly," Jake finally says after a while. "It's the color. That slimy blue-green."

"Yeah," April says. That's the only word she can muster. Lightning flashes over the water far out on the horizon.

"It's fitting," says Jake.

A sudden gust of wind blows April's hair in her face and she brushes it aside, tilting her head a little. "What do you mean?" she asks.

"Ohio. The Midwest. The country. The *planet*. It's so ugly so the lake just fits right in with everything else." He drops his cigarette to the ground and uses his foot to cover it with sand. He lights another and says, "All of it could be beautiful if there weren't any goddamn people to fuck it all up."

April wants to tell him he's too cynical, but that would be profoundly hypocritical; he's heard her speak of her patients…both the ones at the asylum as well as those she sees through her private practice. She wasn't always so pessimistic about mankind, but extended glimpses into pathological human psyches can take a toll on one's sympathies.

"Anyway," Jake says, getting to his feet and picking up his shoes, "I should get going."  April starts to say something, but he speaks first and says, "And…I'm happy for you and Walt. Really, I am."  He gestures with his eyes to the ring on her finger. "I won't be able to make it to the wedding.  I'm sorry."


It's raining and April is sitting in her driveway, watching the wiper blades flick back and forth and back, not wanting to go inside but not knowing why.

She keeps replaying Walt's voicemail.

She listens to his voice telling her he's thinking about her.

That he loves her and hopes she had a good day.

That he wants to have dinner with her tonight, that he wants to talk about the wedding.

He ends it by telling her he loves her again, and it's so genuine, so pure, that it makes her cry.

She keeps playing it until she can't bear it and then she shuts the car off and goes up to her front door, fumbling with her keys, ignoring the bouquet of white roses on the porch that have become soaked and ugly in the rain.  She doesn't look at the waterlogged note to see from whom they came.  Probably

Walt.

    Definitely not Lance.

    Lance isn't sentimental like that.

    As she opens the door and goes inside, she tells herself that she likes that about Lance...his gruff, unromantic and temperamental demeanor, but she can't be sure.

    She doesn't want to acknowledge the fact that she likes him because he's big and muscular and good in bed.

    She doesn't want to acknowledge the fact that she likes him because he treats her like shit.

    Closing the door behind her, April is suddenly cold. *Freezing.*

    It's here.

    It's out.

    It's watching her.

    Not bothering to take off her jacket or shoes, she goes upstairs and crawls into bed and pulls the covers over her head and tries to tell herself it can't see her there.

    But she knows better.

    Her brother calls later that evening and she answers and says, "I can't really talk right now, Derek." She's sitting on her patio sipping brandy and trying not to think. She wouldn't have answered but she knew he would have just kept calling.

"You can never talk," Derek says irritably. "Five minutes, okay? Please."

April doesn't say anything. She takes a sip of her brandy, then another, then downs the rest of it and lights a cigarette.

Derek sighs. "Listen," he says. "Everyone is worried about you."

"I don't know why. Everything is fine." It's forced but she tries not to make it sound that way.

"Walt came over today."

April's fist clenches. She sucks hard on her cigarette and waits for Derek to continue.

"He said it's been over a week since he's heard from you. You're never there when he stops by and you don't answer your cell phone. Every time he calls your office they tell him you're with a patient and that they'll tell you he called."

She knows that's what they tell him. That's what she tells them to tell him.

"I've just been really busy," says April. "I'll call him." She goes inside and into her living room. She sits down on her couch and, deciding she no longer wants the cigarette, crushes it out in the ashtray on the coffee table. It's shaped like a heart and she wonders absently why she would ever buy such an abomination. She wonders what kind of person she used to be, and more so, what kind of person she's become.

There's a pause on the other line. Rustling, and then what sounds like someone else's voice. She can't tell if it's a man or a woman. "You don't sound good," Derek says. "You sound like you're...depressed."

"I'm not depressed, Derek."

Another pause, more rustling, and then, "Are you sure about that?"

"I'm a psychiatrist, in case you've forgotten. I think I'd know if I were depressed." There's venom in her voice so she tries to amend it by saying, "Listen, really, I'm okay. How, um...are you? How is...your life?"

Derek sighs again and then says, "It's fine. Did you hear about Jack?"

"No, what about him?" she asks, not really caring.

"He was in the hospital. He was sleeping with his assistant and her husband beat the shit out of him. He says he might never walk right again."

"That's...a shame. Is he still sober?" Again, not really caring.

"Not anymore. He lost his job and he's living with his mom. He's always drinking and I think he's doing drugs again. You should maybe call him, or something. Get coffee with him. He's not doing so well."

"Yeah, I'll do that," she lies. She really doesn't want to see Jack. She'd probably just end up sleeping with him again and that's not what she wants right now.

After one final, awkward pause, Derek asks, "April, *really*...are you all right?"

"Yes, Derek. I'm more than all right. I'm great. I'm just tired. I'm gonna go, actually. I really need to take a shower."

"Yeah, okay. Well, if you change your mind..."

"Change my mind about *what*, Derek?"

Capitulating, Derek says, "Whatever, I'll let you go. Have a nice night."

April hangs up without replying and then calls Lance.


Lance stands in front of April's bedroom mirror, inspecting the marks on his tan, muscle-rippled back, while April lounges in the tangled sheets upon her bed, watching Lance as she casually picks his skin out from beneath her fingernails.

"I'm bleeding," Lance says.

"Cry about it," April answers, more cruelly than was her intent, and she reaches for the pack of cigarettes on the nightstand.

Lance sits down on the edge of the bed and swipes the pack of cigarettes from April's hand, takes one out and lights it, and then tosses the pack back at her. She looks at him with a strained expression of meek contempt as she lights one herself.

"You've been a real fuckin bitch lately, you know that?" Lance says, turning on the television and switching to ESPN. "The fuck has been up with you?"

April lies back and rests her head on the silk pillow. "Are you really that upset about the scratch marks? I was coming...*hard*...and I..."

"I don't give a fuck about that," says Lance, not taking his eyes from the TV screen. "That's actually kind of hot. I just mean your attitude. You've had a real fuckin attitude and it's been pissing me off."

"I've been...stressed," April says. She glares at his bleeding back and says defiantly, "Deal with it."

Now Lance stands up and looks down at her, face red, jaw clenched. The game has been forgotten. "The fuck did you say to me?" he seethes through his teeth.

Grinning, April says again, "Deal with it. Fucking deal with it. Get the fuck over it. You're..."

He cuts her off by backhanding her across the face. Her head jolts to the side and she cries out.

"Don't you *ever* fucking talk to me like that again," Lance says, his eyes burning.

April slowly turns her head and looks back up at him. "Fuck you," she spits, and he hits her again, harder this time.

"I don't like doing this," Lance says, "but you need to

know your fucking place."

April tenderly touches her fingertips to her reddened cheek and winces. She looks down at her cigarette, which has fallen to the floor and gone out, and for some reason the sight of it brings tears to her eyes and she begins to weep. "Fuck me," she says in between sobs. "Just...shut up and fuck me, okay?"

Lance stares down at her for a few more moments before he violently seizes her throat with one hand and squeezes her breast with the other, and then he complies.

April cries the entire time. She cries hardest when she comes, and isn't able to calm down until it's over and Lance wordlessly dresses himself and then leaves. After that, April just sits there in her bed and feels it watching her, and then she finally begins to laugh.


"There has to be something more than this," April says into her phone. She sits huddled in her bed, phone to her ear, watching the rain slide down the window pane like the black mascara tears that run silently down her stricken face.

"I don't know," she says. "Just something...*more*." She lights a cigarette and then looks down at the crimson lipstick ring around the filter.

"*No*, that's *not* what I mean," she says irritably. "What I *mean* is...I just...Jesus, I don't fucking know. This just can't be *it*."

She listens and watches the smoke drift up to the ceiling that's beginning to yellow.

"Yes," she answers, "I *know* that. But what's your point? What is that going to solve? It's not going to make any of this go away."

She listens again, clutching the phone tight enough to whiten her knuckles, and then replies, "The grime." She looks disgustedly down at her skin. "It won't clear away the *grime*. Don't you *understand*? I'm submerged in it. I'm so fucking deep. I am...too low. I....I have to look up just to see hell."

She pulls the phone away from her ear and looks down at it and realizes that it's dead, and she can't remember how long it's been that way.

The director of the Midian Mental Institution for the Criminally Insane stares tiredly at April and tells her there's nothing he can do.

April stands on the other side of the director's desk, looking down at the clipboard in her hands, biting her lip. "I can't," she says. "Not him. There's a...conflict of interest. It would be...unethical."

The director drums his fat fingers on his desk and says

again, "I'm sorry, but there's really nothing I can do. My hands are tied, here. With Ethan and Kyle both out on leave, I'm incredibly shorthanded. Everyone has to take on extra patients, that's just how things are going to have to go for now. It's not permanent."

"I'm fine with taking on extra patients," April says, trying to keep her voice steady. She sits down in one of the leather chairs across from the director. She puts the clipboard on his desk and folds her hands on her lap and says, "I'll take five more in place of him. Give him to someone else."

The director just keeps shaking his head. "Dr. Diver, please stop making this difficult. All the paperwork has already been done. He's been officially assigned to you." He pauses, shuffles through some folders until he finds what he's looking for and then says, "It says here that he's quite docile. Rarely speaks, even during his weekly therapy sessions. Seems disconnected and perpetually distracted." He looks back up at April and smiles a fake smile. "You'll be fine. And who knows? Maybe you'll be able to make some sort of breakthrough with him. You're a very talented psychiatrist, April. I have faith in you."

"Technically it's against the law," April says quietly.

The director's face darkens and his lips curl into an ugly frown. "And who's going to report us? *You?* Don't test me, April. My buttons don't like to be pushed."

April thinks to herself that there's a fat joke somewhere in there, but she just says, "You misunderstand, sir. I'm just...being precautionary. But..."

"'But' nothing. He's yours. Have a lovely day, Dr. Diver." He slides the clipboard back across the desk and returns to his paperwork, ignoring April's continued presence. After a few moments, she gets up and takes the clipboard and walks out of the director's office.

She tries to tell herself that it's not that big of a deal, but she keeps thinking about the crime scene photos and she has to run to the nearest restroom to vomit and weep.


April sits in the chair with a notebook and a pen and looks at the patient, who's lying on the couch with his hands clasped on his stomach, staring blankly up at the ceiling. It all feels so terribly stereotypical, and she thinks he knows this.

As much as it nauseates her to admit, he's more attractive than she'd remembered, with his hard features and longish wavy dark hair and emerald eyes behind his horn rimmed glasses. Something in April's loins stirs and she crosses her legs and looks out the window.

A long silence passes, and then finally April looks at the tape recorder on the little table next to her and, after a brief moment of deliberation, turns it off.

"They told me you don't say much during these sessions," she says.

The patient doesn't answer; he just keeps staring, seemingly unblinkingly, up at the ceiling.

"But I'm hoping," April goes on, "that you'll have some things to say to *me*."

Still no response.

"I knew Helen Winchester," April says. "She was my friend. She was my fucking *babysitter* when I was a kid."

The patient twitches, and then with slow, languid stiffness, sits up and looks at April. "No she wasn't," he says.

"The *fuck* she wasn't. She used to watch my brother and me every day after school, and she..."

"I believe that she was your babysitter," the patient says, his cold eyes boring straight through April's skull. "But she wasn't your friend. You did not know Helen Winchester." His voice is flat and dead.

April blinks and clenches her fists. "What the fuck is that supposed to mean?"

"It means you did not know Helen. Maybe she was your babysitter. Maybe you thought she was your friend. But you didn't know her."

"You..."

"Do you think that I killed her." There's no inflection in

his voice; his tone is so dry and lifeless that the question comes out sounding like a bored, observatory statement.

April narrows her eyes and taps her pen against the notebook. "Would you be here if you didn't?"

The corners of the patient's mouth twitch slightly, as if a smile rose and died on his lips in the matter of a millisecond. "By the standards of your society, I belong here. But not for murder."

"Then why do you belong here?"

He takes off his glasses and wipes the lenses on the cuff of his sleeve and then puts them back on, eyeing her passively. "I didn't kill Helen."

She opens her mouth to speak and her chest fills with air, readying for an angry outburst, but then the patient says, "Are you happy, Dr. Diver."

The question knocks the wind out of her and she involuntarily slumps a little in her chair. She brushes a lock of hair from her face and says unevenly, "Why would you...ask that?"

"You don't look happy. You look like you're...dead inside."

*That's a good way to put it*, April thinks in spite of herself. *Maybe I am. I need to shower. I'm covered in grime.*

"It amuses me, watching you people," the patient says. "The doctors, the nurses, the orderlies...you're all so miserable.

You're living the only kind of life you know how to, and you are...dissatisfied."

April wants to retort, but she can't, because he's right. In her case, at least, he's right. So instead, she says, "I'm going to...I think I need to up the dosage of your medication."

The patient is unfazed. "You're all trying to make me into some kind of zombie," he says. "All the fucking drugs. But you can't kill me any more than the world already has. I've been dead for a long time." His mouth twitches again, and this time comes closer to a grin, but it is wretched and sinister and it vanishes with merciful brevity. "A long time," he says again. "Just like you."


It's sunny and unseasonably warm but April doesn't feel any better about anything.

She sits across from Walt at a table on the Ladderhouse patio, watching the waitress take another couple's order and wondering if she's prettier than she is.

"You look tired," Walt says. His voice is soft and concerned and this irritates April almost to the point of shrieking, but she forces a smile and tells him she's fine. He looks away and sips his beer, some sort of high-brow hipster specialty brew, and she wants to tell him to stop being such a pretentious pussy and just drink a Budweiser or something, for chrissake, but she just looks away, too.

The restaurant patio overlooks the narrow Villa River and the heavily wooded forest on the opposite side of it, and Walt says, "It's such a pretty view, don't you think?"

With a hand she prays Walt doesn't notice is shaking, April takes a long swig of her vodka gimlet and then says, "Yeah. It's...beautiful."

Walt meets her gaze again and says, "So, um, you've been busy at work?"

April shrugs.

Walt looks down at his lap and says quietly, "They always tell me you're busy when I call you at your office or the hospital."

"I told you not to call me at work."

"You haven't been answering your cell phone."

"Yeah, well, I've...been busy."

The waitress comes over to their table and April still can't figure out if she's prettier. She shifts in her seat and looks over the railing and down at the river and pretends to be deep in thought.

"Are you guys ready to order?" the waitress asks in a cheerful voice that sounds stupid and fake, like a cheerleader out of some dumb teen movie.

"We're just going to stick with the drinks for now, thank

you," Walt answers in a genuinely pleasant tone that April finds even more annoying than the waitress's airheaded squeak.

The waitress says with inflated buoyancy that that's "no problem" and to "just holler if they need her", and April seriously contemplates pitching her glass at that freckly tan face, but it's still half full and that would be a waste.

"What was I saying?" Walt asks April after the waitress bounces jovially away. He sips his beer again but keeps his eyes on April, as if he's afraid of her.

"I don't know," April lies.

They're quiet for a while, just drinking in silence and looking out over the valley. A finch lands on the railing and chirps at Walt, who smiles, and April envisions herself grabbing the bird and stuffing it down her fiancé's throat.

She sighs and lights a cigarette. She stares forlornly at the burning tip and then says, "I really need...to shower."

"You said you showered before coming here. You texted me and said you might be a little late because you had to jump in the shower."

April can't figure out if he's being accusatory, or just innocently confused. Either way, he's right...she *did* shower before coming here. But a fresh, thick layer of sticky grime is once again upon her, had started collecting as soon as she left, and she wants it off her. She scratches at her neck, then her arm, and then says, "I guess I just...need to shower...again."

Walt's face is wrought with concern. "April, I'm really worried, here. You don't seem...yourself. You haven't for a while." It's been much longer than "a while", but April knows he doesn't want to acknowledge that. She almost pities him. Walt says, "Your life is all about diagnosing other people, helping them with *their* problems, and I don't think you take enough time for yourself. Maybe you should...talk to someone."

"Really, I'm fine," April says, flicking ash over the railing. "Really." She reaches for her drink and then suddenly decides she doesn't want it anymore. She wishes she'd thrown it at the waitress.

Walt frowns and replies, "What's that thing you tell your patients when *they* say that *they're* fine?" He thinks for a second, and then remembers and says, "Fucked-up, insecure, neurotic, and emotional, right?"

"Yeah," April answers. "It's just something a professor said in college." She drags deeply from her cigarette and closes her eyes. She feels dizzy but it's not from the nicotine or the alcohol. "It doesn't mean anything."

For some reason she thinks of Jake, and the accident, and all the blood. She thinks of him lying there in the road while she knelt by him, she having sustained a few scratches and scrapes while he had a hunk of metal sticking out of his pelvis. She thinks of the way his eyes looked when she held his hand and told him everything was going to be just fine.

"Ma'am? Excuse me, ma'am?" April opens her eyes and it's the waitress, her brow furrowed unflatteringly. "Ma'am, I'm going to have to ask you not to smoke. Some of the other guests are getting...offended."

April looks around. A group of twenty-somethings sitting a few tables away are watching, their faces scrunched up in disgust. One of them is actually pinching his nose. Another one is puffing from an inhaler.

"Jesus, you've got to be kidding me," April says, glaring at the kids and then at the waitress. "You really can't be serious."

"Please just put it out, April," Walt says. There's no firmness or command in his voice, and April thinks of how Lance would have said it...*Put the goddamn thing out, April, you're making a fucking scene. Don't embarrass me.* She would have preferred that. Walt just sounds like a pussy.

"Ma'am, I'm sorry, but you really can't smoke out here," the waitress says, clearly straining to remain pleasant and to mask her growing irritation.

April takes another hit from the cigarette and then hands it to the waitress. "You put it out," she says. "Just...go away."

The waitress tentatively takes the cigarette, looking at it with exaggerated revulsion, and then scuttles off.

Walt takes a deep breath and runs a hand through his hair, which April thinks is getting too long. And he should shave his beard, too. It's starting to look unruly and gross. "April, you really don't have to be like that. She's just doing her job."

April considers saying something like, "Why are you defending her?" or "Why don't you go marry *her*, if you like her so much," but she doesn't want to be one of those types of girls, because she's *not* one of those types of girls. So instead she stands up, leans over to kiss Walt briefly upon his hairy cheek, and says, "I have to go. I have to go shower. I'm sorry. I'll call you later. After I...shower."

She leaves but doesn't go directly home. She lights a joint when she gets into her car and for a while just drives around getting high and listening to music she doesn't recognize. She doesn't want to go home to that thing but she wants to shower. She knows it will probably watch her shower, as it often does. She smokes another joint and gets lost and then calls someone and cries for a while, even after the other person has hung up. Maybe the other person never even answered.

*Maybe I'm losing it.*

She thinks of the patient and then muses, *Maybe I'm dead.*

So much grime.

All of the self-contrived problems of the "sick", all their

whining complaints and pitiful lamentations, their bleating pleas for a pill-shaped panacea to a chronic condition that can be diagnosed only as *life*, and whose prognosis is always nothing less than certain *death*...all of this grime, all of it and more, sliding from April's body and swirling around the shower drain before being mercifully sucked down into the abyssal sewers beneath the shrieking pit of retarded children that is the World of Man.

The steaming water pelts her with its forceful urgency, bursting forth from the shining chromium nozzle like revitalizing rainfall upon a barren desert wrought with drought and decay. She is purified once more, or at least as much as is possible at this stage in her rapid descent into the very ailment she claims to treat.

Salty tears mix with the water streaming down her face. From the stereo in her living room comes Framing Hanley's "Built for Sin", just barely audible over the sound of the shower. Her house is empty. If music plays and only Dr. April Diver can hear it, does it still make a sound?

When she is at last cleansed and the water runs cold, she twists the nozzle and for a few long minutes just stands dripping in the tub, shivering in spite of herself, listening to the droplets of moisture plink down onto the porcelain. Everything else is silent; the music has stopped, leading her to believe it was indeed never playing in the first place.

Or that something turned it off.

This all feels eerily familiar. Like *déjà vu*, but worse.

She tries to hear her heartbeat and cannot, and two delicate fingers pressed to her thin, faintly pulsing wrist is her only confirmation of her continued feeble existence. A brief look at the razor on the edge of the tub opens a world of possibilities, but only for a moment, for the thought is as fleeting as the glance itself.

She gets out of the shower and dries herself off.

She can already feel the grime beginning to collect again.

## **Pleasant Times Away from Home**

People like explanations. They like things to fit into a nice, neat package, without exception. No inexplicable mysteries, no bizarre phenomena. Just clear and succinct clarifications, and nothing more or less.

These same qualifications apply to serial killers.

People *love* sentimental sob stories to go along with the serial killers they love to hate; it makes it easier to deal with the atrocities that these murderers commit. They like to hear that these killers had heinous childhoods, that they were abused, that they experienced some unspeakable horror that screwed with their inner mechanics and transformed them into monsters.

They *don't* like it when there is no clear-cut explanation for a serial killer's malevolence, which is why Sterling McPleasant was such a despised man in American society. He came from a Catholic upbringing, raised by a family with intensely moralistic values that gave him no motivation to do the awful things he did.

No, Sterling McPleasant was born as a bad man in a world that liked to think it was good, and he didn't *need* motivation. No more than a person needs any motivation other than thirst to drink, no motivation other than hunger to eat. It was part of *him*, and he had no reservations about the person he was.

\*\*\*

By the time the police arrived at Sterling's house to investigate the crime scene in his sister's bedroom, he was already miles away, huddled in a cramped railcar surrounded by crates and watching the landscape rush by him. It would be years before the law ever caught up.

Rachel McPleasant lay in her bed, her sheets doused with blood, naked except for a torn, skimpy brassiere. She had bite marks on her arms and breasts, bite marks that had torn away bits of flesh.

"Any suspects?" Officer Lyon asked Detective DeMint, looking at the corpse with sick revulsion.

The detective shook his head, walking slowly around the bloody bed and biting his lip. "The parents have a solid alibi, and the brother was at a friend's house."

"Where's the brother now?"

"Still at his friend's. He hasn't been told yet."

Lyon rubbed his tired eyes and turned away. "Christ, DeMint, this is a fucking mess. How old was the poor girl?"

"Sixteen. I've seen her before…her family goes to the same church as mine. Pretty girl. Well, she *had* been a pretty girl before she got her face bashed in with a pipe wrench. My guess is that it was a classmate, probably an outcast, who lusted after her. He probably sneaked into the house while the parents were at dinner, killed her, and then raped her. CSU said the rape occurred postmortem."

"Goddamn," Lyon breathed. "I swear to Christ, these kids just keep getting more and more fucked up. I blame the media."

"Blame whatever you want," said DeMint. "Doesn't change anything."

Despite the buzzing in his head, which was always there, McPleasant felt good. He'd planned this for months, and he'd gotten away with it. Now he was free, free to do whatever he pleased and turn his gleeful malice towards the rest of the world.

His sister had only been the beginning. Being but thirteen years old, he had his whole life ahead of him, and he was going to make the absolute best of it.

The train began to slow, so McPleasant stood up and stretched his aching joints. He then moved to the opening of the railcar to peek out, and he smiled. The train was nearing a supply depot, but it was in the middle of a dense forest with no signs of civilization. He couldn't have asked for a better place to disembark.

Humming softly to himself, he grabbed his pack and hopped off the train, bounding nimbly into the woods. Walking felt lovely after four hours in a crouched position, and the air smelled of crisp leaves and early morning dew. The sun had not yet risen, but he could see perfectly. The darkness was his friend, his lover, his partner in crime. It embraced him like no human could, and it accepted him in every way that society would not. In the dark, the buzzing wasn't quite as loud.

He walked without slowing for an hour or two, and as the first rays of sun began to stab through the forest's canopy, McPleasant spotted a young deer with an injured leg. It was dragging itself pitifully through the bushes, blood trickling from what appeared to be a bite wound on its ankle. When it became aware of McPleasant's presence it quickened its pace a little, but it was not capable of moving any faster than McPleasant could at a slow jog.

He'd already taken the meat cleaver from his backpack. It was still speckled with his sister's blood, and he *could* have wiped it off, but he thought having a bloodstained weapon made him look more professional, like a *real* serial killer.

He spent an hour with the deer. He hadn't had as much time with his sister as he would have liked, so he did everything to the deer that he hadn't gotten to do to her. He hacked its head open, giggling at the loud *thuck* noises, and scooped handfuls of its brains out of its fractured skull. He examined the pinkish brain matter, turning it over in his hands and squishing it with his fists. He took a small bite of it, but it tasted foul so he spat it back out and wiped his mouth before moving on to the animal's stomach. He used the knife to cut a long, thick slice in its belly, and then reached inside and felt its warm, slippery innards.

"Fuck," said McPleasant aloud, liking the way it sounded. "Cunt. Cunty cunt cunt." Curse words had always fascinated him, and he let out a string of his favorite profanities as he continued to butcher the deer.

When it was no more than an unrecognizable hunk of bloody flesh, he attempted to copulate with it. When this proved to be boring, he pulled his pants back up and resumed his trek through the wilderness.

He hiked for most of the day, never tiring, until he came upon a small cottage in a vast clearing. It was constructed entirely of logs, and wisps of white smoke billowed from the short chimney. As he approached the cabin, he caught a whiff of the aromatic scent of a freshly-prepared dinner. He was hungry, and he didn't want to go through his granola bars too quickly, so he jogged up to the house and rapped loudly on its front door. A golden plaque was nailed above the door, which read, "The Humble Abode of Walden Thoreaugood."

After a few short moments, the door was opened by a short, thin, smiling man with tousled hair and a scruffy black beard. "Hello, there, young lad," the man said, beaming. "What are you doing here out in the woods all by your lonesome?"

McPleasant, who had never been good with words, said simply, "Hiking."

"Well, you look mighty tired. I just cooked dinner for myself, and if you're hungry I certainly wouldn't mind the company." He opened the door wider and stepped aside, gesturing for McPleasant to enter. He complied without a word and set his pack down on the floor, quickly checking that he hadn't missed anything when he'd wiped his hands clean in the pond he'd stumbled upon a quarter mile or so back.

"My name is Walden Thoreaugood," said the man, "and this is my...*experiment*, of sorts. I'm so sick of civilization, all the computers and cell phones and such, so I've come out here to live a simpler and quieter life."

"Okay," said McPleasant, looking around at the small cottage. The furniture was very basic and makeshift, and the entire interior bore no signs of the twenty-first century. It was peculiar, but there was a hot and steaming turkey on the table, so McPleasant didn't really mind.

As they ate, Walden regarded McPleasant with kind eyes and said, "Where do you live, son? Anywhere close by?"

"No," McPleasant replied, shoving a forkful of turkey into his mouth and washing it down with a gulp of water.

Walden blinked, never shedding that warm and ridiculous grin, and said, "All right, I understand...you don't want to tell me where you live because I'm a stranger, right? Smart boy. Your parents must have taught you well."

McPleasant snickered, thinking of his dead and maimed sister, and ate another bite of turkey.

"You go hiking out here often? I get visitors from time to time, but never someone so young. I'm guessing you don't come out this way too much, right?"

"Nope."

Walden nodded slowly. "You aren't much of a talker, are you?"

"Nope."

"That's all right, son. I can do enough talking for the both of us. See, people used to tell me all the time that my idea of living out here was ridiculous. They said it'd get me killed, one way or another. People aren't meant to live like this, they said. Well, look at me now. I've been out here for almost two years, and I've been doing just fine. Shows *them*. You know, I *know* how to live, you know? They don't, and that's fine. I don't mind. Really, I don't. People can take what they want from my belief system, my little 'experiment,' if you will. I'm not really trying to prove anything. Honestly, I'm not. I just want to, you know, *do*. You know? I want to be who I am and not let what anybody thinks keep me from, you know, being who I am.
"And speaking of individuality, would you just *look* at how conformist everyone has become? Look at everyone dressing

similarly, talking similarly, *living* similarly. I'm so *sick* of the similarity in the world, you know, kid? *Sick* of it. Of course, I don't blame the people of society. And I guess you could say I don't really blame society *itself*, either. It's not really a matter of blaming, when you get right down to it, because blaming doesn't change anything. It's a matter of just, you know, *being*. You know what I mean, right? Of course you do. Just like you know about, say, computers. Don't even get me *started* on computers. They're taking over the *world*, son! I mean, they're *everywhere*, you know? Of course you do. You're a smart boy." He smiled and took a long swig of water, sloshing it around in his mouth and grinning stupidly. "Let me tell you something else, boy…there's no *modesty* anymore. I mean, look at the way the girls *dress*, for God's sake! Just *look*! It's *appalling*! And on television, in movies, in music…it's all about, well, 'it.' Dirty things, you know, son? You *know*?"

Walden continued to talk inanely throughout the rest of the meal, and continued on even after they'd finished, but the buzzing was loud enough for McPleasant to block a lot of it out. But by the time Walden finally got up to take the dishes out to the pond, it was dark, and McPleasant wanted to kill him. He was tiresome and annoying, like so many of the other abhorrent adults McPleasant had encountered during his life. The difference now, though, was that he could do something about it. The others, he'd just had to tolerate them. Not this man. Out in the wilderness, no civilization…no one would know. So as he awaited Walden's return, he crouched under the table with the knife clutched in both hands.

When Walden returned, it seemed as though he was unaware of the fact that McPleasant was not in sight. As soon as the door opened, he was talking again.

"Oh, the *rain!*" he exclaimed, shaking his mane of rain-soaked hair and stomping his wet shoes before bustling into the tiny kitchen to put the dishes away. "You, being a smart boy and all, *must* know the glorious wonders of the rain, the rapturous rain! The way it makes the trees glisten with sparkling moisture, the way it cloaks the leaves in jackets of natural perspiration, the way it makes Mother Nature herself *sing* an exultant chorus of mellow magic…*surely* you must know. Oh, how it just makes me *swell* with bliss!"

He came back out of the kitchen, still unaware that McPleasant was hunkered beneath the table, preparing to spring out and take his prey. "You know, boy, there's something about nature itself that makes me just want to *explode* with excitement, you know? That is *undeniably* my most favorite aspect of my time out here. Sure, I love the seclusion, the escape from society, but it's *nature* that really takes the cake you know?" After this last statement, he turned to face the window so he could gaze out at his beloved rain. It was then that McPleasant pounced.

When the blade buried itself in the side of the recluse's neck, it made a pleasingly loud *shuk!* sound and sent blood the color of raspberries squirting onto the rain-streaked glass. Walden tried to scream, but all that escaped his lips was a wet, gagging groan. McPleasant wrenched the knife free, letting forth a thick freshet of redness that stained his shirt and spattered the floorboards. He fell to his knees, his dying, bewildered eyes reflecting in the window, and McPleasant finished him off by driving the cleaver deep into the top of his skull. The impact killed him instantly, and he fell to his side at McPleasant's feet, pink and scarlet fluids dripping from the wound in his head.

For the next few hours, McPleasant hewed Walden's body apart, lathering himself in the blood and intestines and haphazardly throwing strips of flesh at the wall so he could watch them stick there and slide down, leaving long red trails. He used the knife to peel Walden's face like an orange, and then chopped at his teeth and sawed out his wretched tongue that had so incessantly wagged throughout the course of the night. He eventually grew tired, and he decided to finish with his bloody project in the morning. There was a small cot in the corner of the house that reeked of sweat, but it was a bed, so McPleasant slept.

\* \* \*

Two days later, his feet kicked comfortably up on the hotel room coffee table, McPleasant surfed absently through television channels. The previous tenant of the room lay lifeless on the floor a few feet away, his head cleaved open and his arm broken in several places.

"This is how it's gonna be," McPleasant said, to no one in particular. "From now on, this is how it's gonna be." He sighed contentedly. Killing, for him, was like drinking water. Before his sister, he'd just killed small animals, and that had been like sucking on ice cubes in terms of quenching thirst. But *after* killing his sister, he'd felt completely rejuvenated. Like taking huge mouthfuls of the purest spring water. Fornicating with her corpse had been delightful, as well, but the killing, as Walden would have said, really took the cake.

And now that he'd gotten a real taste of killing, he wasn't going to stop. Now that he'd drunk actual water, he was done with ice cubes. It was crisp, natural water from here on out.

He looked back over at the dead man and whistled through his teeth. It was only just beginning.

Because humans, normal or crazy, killer or victim, are all the same.

And they all get thirsty.

## To the Face

This is not a cry for help.

If I'm clear about one thing, and one thing only, let it be that...

This is not a cry for help.

First let me say this: I don't believe in the phenomenon known as the "suicide attempt". Allow me to elaborate. If you *really* want to kill yourself, you're going to fucking kill yourself.

Period.

End of story.

When life becomes such a burdensome tribulation that the only solution is death, don't you think a person would make *damn* sure that the death was done right? A man's final act in life will never be half-hearted. Make no mistake; a person who wants to die *will* die.

And I want to fucking die.

I'm not a sympathy-seeking attention whore.

I'm not a moody teenager who just wants to be noticed.

I don't listen to Hawthorne Heights.

Suicide is not a fucking fashion statement.

Prescribe me Prozac. Prescribe me Zoloft. Prescribe me Paxil. Cymbalta, Abilify, Celexa, Lexapro, Effexor, Wellbutrin, Elavil. Prescribe me Pristiq, Sensoval, Remeron. Put me in therapy, put me in hospitals, put me in psych wards. Send me to support groups, weekend retreats, seasonally-themed mixers.

Medicate me.

Rehabilitate me.

*Fix* me.

Right? *Right?* That's the answer, isn't it? *Isn't it?* Not feeling well? Feeling kind of *blue*? Don't worry, we have a *pill* for that!

Fuck off.

I've got pills, too, now that you mention it. Set out before me, on this table, all a part of my farewell gesture to the world. I've got Valium. I've got Xanax. I've got Vicodin. Percocet, Percodan, Klonopin, Ultram, Demerol, Ryzolt, Metanor. I've got ProSom, Librium, Ambien. All these pills, all dumped into a big heaping pile in the center of the table, hundreds of capsules and tablets compiled into a miniature Everest of primarily-schedule-I pharmaceuticals in my very own dining room.

And if all of those aren't convincing enough, I've got some razor blades, a kitchen knife, a box cutter, a letter opener, and…my personal favorite…the grand finale, the big shebang, drumroll *please*…a sawed-off twelve-gauge shotgun.

Yeah.

I plan to do this right.

But why, Nameless Narrator, *why*? You've got so much to *live* for! You've got your whole *life* ahead of you!

Yes, a *reason*. Everyone always wants a fucking *reason*.

Well, pick one. Any of them. It doesn't make a difference to me. Throw it on the board and see if it sticks.

My girlfriend dumped me.

I lost my job.

My spouse is cheating on me.

Those are the common ones, right? Like I said, pick one. Check yes or no. Select the response that BEST answers the question. Please do not fill in more than one bubble.

Right, well, they're all the same, aren't they? In the end, is there really any difference?

I'm depressed.

No one loves me.

My daddy molested me.

There, more fan favorites. Knock yourself out, go crazy.

Crippling debt.

*Blam.*

Diagnosed with terminal illness.

*Blam.*

Substance abuse problems.

*Blam.*

Dead lover.

*Tie the noose.*

Economic recession.

*Stand on the chair.*

Favorite sports team never wins.

*JUMP.*

You get the idea.

All of the above, none of the above, it doesn't matter. All that matters is…wait for it…*wait for it…*

I want to fucking die.

And?

Oh, yeah…

This is not a cry for help.

I've got Slipknot playing from my stereo because there's something obnoxious and poetic about that and I'm an angry romantic at heart. Just because I'm not doing this for attention doesn't mean I can't be a little dramatic about it.

Mr. Beam helps me swallow the first handful of pills. "Thank you, Lord Jim," I tell him, and then light a cigarette. Camels, unfiltered. I get tobacco leaves in my mouth and nigger-lip the paper, but for once it doesn't seem like that big of a deal. Impending death has a nice way of putting things in perspective.

I take another swig from the bottle, for the sake of good measure, and stare at the wall. I ash on the carpet because, let's be honest, what the fuck do I care at this point? What's my landlord going to do? Evict me?

I hope he's the one who finds me.

I hope the stink of my putrid expiration looms over this godforsaken hole for the rest of eternity.

I hope there are maggots in my skin when they zip me up in rubber and cart me off to the morgue.

Sounds kind of extreme, right? Like, why not just shoot myself and be done with it? Why go to all this trouble to wreak havoc upon my body before finally doing the actual deed?

I'll fucking tell you why.

My body is the last and only thing I can rightfully destroy. I must enact all of this hate upon something before I go. I can't die with all of this inside me. I have to let it out. I don't claim to have any idea what's on the other side, or if there's even anything at all, but if there *is* something, I really don't want to cross over with a bunch of pent-up rage.

Kind of like, I don't know, jacking off before you go to a strip club so you don't do anything embarrassing.

But no, this isn't my ideal way to do things.

I swallow another handful of pills and light the joint I've rolled for the occasion.

No, my body is not my ideal target. I don't have any *real* desire to use myself as a living voodoo doll, it's not what I *truly* want to do, but I'm doing it because it's all I *can* do.

So, what do I *want* to do?

Glad you asked.

I want to set fire to everything that was ever sacred. I want the whole world to feel my hate. I want all of them to be consumed by it, *sick* with it.

Hit the bottle, hit the joint, tilt my head back, *exhale*. I can feel it all settling in now. It tingles.

I want to skull-fuck sanctity. I want to tear the tongues from every mouth that utters promises of hope and happiness and then choke them all with their own putrid shit.

I want to beat the brains out of retarded children and dance to the chorus of their braying screams.

I want to castrate all the happy husbands and make them watch while I rape their blushing brides with dildos wrapped in barbed wire.

I want to carve up the faces of all the beautiful people and fill their big homes with kerosene. I want to impale the politicians with the flags of their people and laugh when they puke blood all over their taxpayer-paid-for suits.

Dragging the razor blade slowly across my wrist, I smile at the blood that seeps up and out, slithering down my arm and plinking onto the table and the linoleum floor.

Drip.

Drip.

*Drip*.

Dripdripdripdripdripdripdrip.

I want to bomb a children's cancer ward while adorned in red and white candy stripes.

Swallowing some more pills, gulping more liquor, there's a buzzing in the back of my head and my limbs feel heavy.

Gravity is getting confused. I am confused.

I want to douse nursing home residents in gooey napalm.

I want to free zoo beasts from their cages and sic them upon their captors.

I want everyone to just fucking *die.*

I want to see the world smothered in a holocaust of madness and devastation and disease. I want to dismantle society brick by brick and grin as it collapses into smoldering ruin. Burn, burn, burn, burn. I want to stand upon ash and cinder and declare myself God of the Nothing.

I want fire.

I want death.

I want an *end.*

I am God's unwanted bastard child, and, more than anything, I want to cut Him down for abandoning me.

The kitchen knife looks really attractive right now, like a sleek, deadly pinup girl, so I seize it by the waist and drive her pointed face into my groin.

Savagely sharp teeth biting into my genitals, this beautiful beauty queen delivers me more pain than I thought was possible. I clamp down on my tongue. Blood spurts out of my mouth as I scream. I twist the knife, push her head down harder, gasp and wheeze and reach desperately for more pills. Chew, chew, chew, *breathe,* it's just pain, it will soon be gone, it is to be temporary and brief, it's just pain, chew, chew, crunchcrunchcrunch grab bottle tip swish swallow, blood and alcohol seeping out from between my trembling lips.

Destruction of self is the only way to freedom. The Buddhists say something like that.

I'm running with it.

Cheeks sticky with tears, throat scratchy from screaming, but even those sensations are fleeting. The drugs are taking hold. Everything is getting fuzzy and even the worst of the pain is ebbing.

Death is coming.

I can feel it. By taking the power of death, by *becoming* it, my life is in my control for the first time since my tragic conception. I am now in charge of my fate.

People kill themselves because God never does it soon enough.

Uncaring, self-righteous bastard.

I pop more pills.

Suddenly I'm standing in the kitchen, clutching the edge of the sink with one hand, other hand holding…a cheese grater? Why a cheese grater? I don't remember coming in here, I don't remember getting the cheese grater or why I thought I needed it. I didn't even know I owned a cheese grater.

I take it to my face and start rubbing. *Grating.* I can't feel anything. I know it's working because blood is pouring down into the sink and swirling around the drain, leaving brown stains on the steel in its wake, but I don't actually feel it. This excites me and I grate harder, shaving away bits of flesh that fall like snow from my bleeding face. My legs are wobbly and weak and I know they're going to give out soon so I really go to town, so hard that I can *almost* feel it, but then out go my legs and…fade to black, everything disappears for a while until I come back, lying on the linoleum, laughing hysterically. I touch my fingers to my ruined face but there's no sensation there, which is disappointing.

Back at the table, everything seems a little clearer, not much but a little, and I wouldn't even think the episode in the kitchen had happened if it wasn't for the blood spilling onto the table and the gore-smeared cheese grater lying on the floor a few yards away. Blood from my forehead is seeping into my eyes and I have to keep rubbing them. Speaking of blood, holy shit, there's a ton of it on my crotch and running down the legs of my jeans. How the fuck did I even manage to walk to the kitchen? And seriously, why did I go there in the first place? Things to ponder in the afterlife, if there is one.

Here's to hoping there isn't.

I want only oblivion.

My head lolls and all the feeling in my body is pretty much completely gone. That's how I'm able to pick up the supermodel knife and start scalping myself. I saw at my cheese-grated forehead right where my hairline stops, and I just saw and saw and saw, not feeling anything. After I've sawed about three-quarters of the way back, I'm able to peel the rest of it off, and a big strip of hairy skin comes away in my hand. I let it fall and the sound is a lot like dropping a wet rag on a hard floor.

The blood's really coming now, all down my face and the sides of my head, collecting in my ears.

*This* is destruction of the self. Fuck you, Buddha, you ain't got shit.

I gobble some more pills, stab myself in the face a couple times just because I can. Hack at my arms with the razor blade. I take up the knife once more and *one slice two slice three slice four* and my nose comes off, flopping down in my soaked lap. *Five slice six slice seven slice more* and my right ear follows. Then I use the knife to gouge out my left eye, which I then squeeze between my fingers until it pops and spews milky white fluid straight up in the air like a gushing ejaculation. I toss away the knife and cut off my lips with the box cutter.

Still more pills. Chomp chomp chomp, swallow, almost choke, swallow swallow all gone, we're good.

I notice for the first time that there's puke everywhere, and the bottle of Jim Beam is empty and lying on its side. I don't remember finishing it, nor do I remember vomiting. The puke, though…it's literally *everywhere*, all over the floor, all over the table, all over *me*. I can't smell it because, guess what, I don't have a fucking nose. Put that in your fucking pipe and smoke it,

Michael Jackson.

I take some more pills because I don't know how many I threw up, but it shouldn't be a big deal because whatever's left in me, combined with the blood loss, is definitely taking its toll and I don't think I've got much longer left. I'd love to give some Shakespearean soliloquy about the meaning of life and death but apparently I've cut out my tongue, too, because it's sitting there on the table next to the letter opener. I only notice this after I've wiped more blood from my eye.

I almost fall out of my chair. That's bad. If I fall, I don't know that I'll be able to get up. And I might be fucking *gone*, fucking *checked out*, but I still want to finish with a bang so I best get to it. Hands slippery with blood, I take up the gun and shove its twin barrels in my mouth. I wish I could tell you what it tastes like but I don't have a tongue, remember. Sorry, folks. Oh well. I can imagine. I imagine it tastes like a rabbit, all furry and shit frolicking through industrial parks and soaring soaring soaring like eagles like eagles and there are hobbits and shit, too, and dragons and sleeping princesses and that bitch with the funky hat, let it rain, let it rain.

Sing.

Mom's here, hey mom.

Dancing cats with monocles and candy canes like batons. Let Jesus fuck you, let Jesus fuck you. Pea soup, head spins. Lincoln screaming DO IT DO IT DO IT throwing golf balls at me, pissing on jellyfish.

    Hammer falls and bathroom stalls and wooden cabinets toilet plunger ghosts purple fedoras HAPPY BIRTHDAY black guitar case salt rock salt rock salt lamp bottles of oil aloe lotion Magnesium pills wristwatch wristwatch Bic book wire through cheek and gum fuzzy SLIPPERS blinds up down nine four one RING chug chug jug-a-lugga ding-DONG tall tower fan stripes and checkers and custom Las Vegas propane cylinders military uniforms military FACTION here we go here we go I feel it coming little bits of CLARITY here we

    Eyes cast up at the…no, *eye*, as in singular, other one's gone to Poland, Lou Gehrig style…eyes cast up at the…no, fuck, dammit, just one eye, just one, singular, other one is fuck fuck fuck *fucking* your *mother* up at the ceiling and I'm thinking, I win, I win, I win, I don't know what I've won but I definitely won and the gun's in my mouth my finger is on the winner winner winner ding ding ding have a pink cigar and

## Sick Again

Vicodin, Percocet, Oxycontin, liquid codeine…nail clippers, Q-tips, chewable Flintstone vitamins…Excedrin, toothpaste, eye droppers, cherry-flavored antacids (but no warm milk or laxatives to speak of)…tweezers, a woman's disposable razor…an empty tube of Vaseline, a rolled-up dollar bill, a box of Trojans, a brown vial of expired amoxicillin.

These are the items in the asshole's medicine cabinet. I look at them, and I smile a smug little grin; glancing inside a man's medicine cabinet is one of the few great ways to truly violate what little privacy he maintains. Men, by nature, are largely shameless creatures with a tragically limited understanding of discretion. That being said, when uninvited eyes fall upon the intimate objects behind that little mirrored door, the intruder becomes very aware of a line that has been crossed.

I am aware of that line, but I am free from any sense of guilt. The way I see it, the moment this guy decided to fuck my wife was the moment he was relieved of his privacy privileges. You have to seize opportunities for small victories such as this when they present themselves.

I close the small door to the medicine cabinet, my cold and deadened heart warmed slightly by the thought of a man who simultaneously abuses prescription drugs and eats vitamins shaped like cartoon characters that nobody even remembers anymore.  The humor of it passes quickly, though; now all I can think about is how my *wife*, the center of my existence and the woman to whom I have tethered every fabric of my being, could possibly be inclined to *fuck* someone like this.

I start to turn away, but am stopped by the face sneering out at me from the unfeeling glass of the mirror, a face that is not mine but instead hers.  Her eyes are cold and shallow, and it is only in them that I see my own reflection, pale and shivering and drunk, the sole imperfection beset her horribly flawless face.  She flashes a beautiful and terrible smile, a smile full of perceived promises and cool, unfeeling deadness.

"Look at yourself," says the phantasm in the mirror, her voice seething and disgusted.  "Look at what you're doing.  *Remember* this, if you ever grow the fuck up."

It is my voice as much as it is hers, goading me, taunting me, *conflicting* me.  I look down at the bottle of Southern Comfort in my quavering hand and see myself smashing it into the mirror, obliterating her jeering face, but I am more afraid of a shattered, useless bottle of liquor than I am of her.  There is nothing she can do to me that cannot be numbed.  I...have...an *escape*.

"You are a coward," she derides, beaming with satisfaction.  "You are incapable of doing anything alone."

Again I briefly give vague consideration to the notion of

destroying the mirror, but instead elect to drink deeply from the bottle and squeeze shut my throbbing eyes, thinking she will remain without them where she belongs.

But then there's that image again, ever persistent and inescapable...their writhing, sweating bodies entwined together, her euphoric moans overlapping with his brutish grunts. Their movements are aggressive and lacking any notion of passion, making them seem less like lovers and more like animals in heat. I have not yet beheld the likeness of the man whose apartment in which I am currently trespassing, so in my imagination he currently resembles the grotesque offspring of an irradiated pig and a diseased mule.

As is to be expected...*par for the course,* as we Americans so lovingly say...a familiar twinge of nausea ensnares my stomach the second that the vile scene begins to unfold inside of my woefully troubled mind, where it will continue to play on repeat for some time. This is standard operating procedure.

I close my eyes and grip the edges of the bathroom counter, taking deep breaths and waiting for the sick feeling to pass. There is poison in my veins, a burning, corrosive acid that circulates through my body, contaminating my blood with what feels like a thousand lifetimes of betrayal and sorrow. This is what love does to you...not necessarily at first, but if you wait around to get your heart broken, it becomes a ruthless toxin that will eventually drag you into a state of rabid delirium, and then the next thing you know you're stumbling into a twenty-something's shitty little apartment with murder on your mind.

The best antidotes are poisons in and of themselves, so I take another long swig of my long-beloved SoCo and let its warmth flush the worst of her venom from my burning, bubbling blood, allowing the alcohol to slurp up the poison into its unprejudiced mouth among endless rows of razor-like teeth. This is not the healthy answer, but it is the best one.

I leave the bathroom and walk out into the living room, where I sit down on the couch and look around slowly. There's a boxy old TV with some sort of video game device beneath it, and a large stereo system in the corner, equipped with turntables and a microphone. Posters of mostly-naked starlets hang on the walls, and several issues of *Playboy* and *Penthouse* lie scattered about on the coffee table.

*What the fuck did you see in this juvenile douchebag? How could you come here and be compelled to desecrate our marriage by hopping in bed with someone like this? You're better than this...*I'm better than this...*if you* had *to cheat, why not do it with someone who isn't a pathetic stereotype of a randy American asshole who probably spends his days playing video games and jacking off? Why not have a little fucking self-respect?*

Raising the bottle to my face, I am dismayed by its emptiness...it had been half full just moments ago in the bathroom, and somewhere between there and here, then and now, I had finished it despite my lack of knowledge of doing so. I can *almost* feel that which I must have drank sitting pleasantly in my chest, but that could have been there before, and it is no longer noticeable enough to be worthy of explicit mention.

I stand up and go into the kitchen, which is a mess. There are heaps of dirty dishes in the sink, empty Bud Light cans hither and thither, and there's a half-eaten slice of pizza lying on the floor. I open the refrigerator and find it filled with more Bud Light and pizza, a couple two-liters of Mountain Dew, and a huge tray of Jell-O shots. I shake my head and turn away, not bothering to close the refrigerator door.

Her voice returns, this time pleading and repentant. "Don't do this," she begs. "I made a mistake, I wasn't in the right place, I was *mixed up*. You have to understand. I *love* you. We can get through this. I *want* to get through this. I can't lose you…not after everything, not after all *this*."

Debilitated, I collapse against the wall, grappling futilely for support but all the while sinking down, down, down into the sea of linoleum and its urging waves of despair. I cannot see without her…I am blind and there is darkness, so much darkness, but simultaneously I can see *everything*. It is all there before me, and it is hideous, and that is precisely why I must do what I came here to do.

I force myself to shaky, unsure feet and start opening random drawers and pawing through them until I find one filled with various eating utensils and cutlery. I select the longest knife and test its sharpness against my thumb, smiling at the little stab of pain and the bead of blood that eagerly rushes to the surface of the cut. Still grinning, I stick the knife in the waistband of my jeans.

I guess, when you get down to it, this isn't about revenge; if I *really* wanted to make this guy suffer, I would let him live out his wretched, pitiful life to the end of his days. Unfortunately for him, though, that isn't my objective. Vengeance doesn't interest me, but freedom does. This is all about liberation…liberating myself from the knowledge of his existence, liberating my wife from the ability to go back to him, and liberating the world from his parasitic presence among people who actually matter. More than anything, I'm liberating *him* from *himself*, and for that I should be awarded, praised, *accepted*. Everybody benefits from this outcome. This is negative eugenics at its absolute best.

I can see her so clearly…gorgeous, divine, untarnished by the grinding rust of perpetual life…she is everything I thought I would never have, everything I *could* have had but never will. I had her in a conventional sense, but I never *really* had her…I could tell myself that because of that I never really lost her, either, but that would be a lie. Years spent by her side, in her bed, her *heart*…all for naught, all because of my own fucked-up deficiency of a straight, legitimate consciousness. I deserve her absence because of my own. Things are this way because I made them so; to fault her for everything is to lie to the self, to deny the reality I seek so desperately to escape. I sought it through her, to no avail, and so I must turn elsewhere.

This is where I find myself.

This is where I begin.

This is where I end.

Next stop...*last* stop...the asshole's bedroom. As I walk down the hallway towards the partially ajar door, my heart palpitates with anticipation. Everything in my life, and everything in his, has led to this. It will be in this man's bedroom that our universes will converge in a culmination of blood and emotion. He no doubt thinks his future holds in store for him great wealth and success and a playground of promiscuous women, but no, he will fulfill his purpose tonight, in this shitty apartment, his fate now resting at the end of the knife in my waistband. His part in my wife's adulterous doings has made him mine; all that he is, was, or ever will be now belongs entirely to me.

And lately, I've been making a habit of destroying my possessions.

I creep quietly through the door and into the guy's bedroom, and I have to swallow a harsh laugh. If the rest of the apartment didn't accurately sum up this piece of shit, his bedroom certainly does. It smells strongly of sex and beer and piss...maybe even a hint of my wife's perfume, but that could be in my imagination. Mounted over his bed (a *water*bed in the shape of a heart, no less) is a huge poster of Ricky Rampage, rocking out on a stage with shooting pyrotechnics, wearing nothing but a tattered British flag around his waist, topless women bowing down at his feet. Here's to role models, kids.

Dirty laundry is strewn all over the stained carpet, and there's a small garbage can to my left that's filled with used condoms and more beer cans. On the table beside his bed is a magnum of Sky vodka and an alarm clock shaped like a naked woman. A wobbly ceiling fan whirls loudly overhead.

*How did you feel when you first came here? Did you gaze upon this mess and find something enthralling about it? No, I don't think so. I think you were disgusted with his misogynistic possessions and the disorderly state of his apartment...I think you found it revolting, but then he took off his shirt and you forgot all about it. And the rest...is...history.*

I take a few steps forward. Moonlight spills in through the window, illuminating the heart-shaped bed and the man sleeping in it. Seeing my wife's lover for the first time, my muscles go rigid with hate and my mouth fills with bitter saliva. I am full of resolve. I will not leave this room until the man in that bed has been robbed of his life in the same way that he robbed me of the woman I love.

"Last chance. Turn around. We can still be *something*.

Everything doesn't have to be for nothing."

My eyes are waterlogged with soggy tears of grief and self-pity. She can whisper and talk and vow all she likes, but I am here, I have come this far, and I see no exit door. Five to one, one in five, no one here gets out alive.

I take the knife from my jeans and advance closer until I'm standing over the bed, my shadow falling over the sleeping man within it.

He even sleeps like an asshole. Arms and legs splayed out, mouth agape, chest rising and falling in rhythm with his loud snores...he's a caricature of my expectations. He's maybe twenty-five, at the oldest, his body lean and tan and rippled with muscle. Tattooed on his shoulder is a tiger-striped jolly roger that's surrounded by a circle of inverted pentagrams. His hair is dark and shaggy, making him look a little bit like Russell Brand, whom I never thought was that good looking, anyway.

"We could have been something...we could have been *everything*. We were almost there, but I fucked up a little bit. Everything is an experience, right? We...we can't end it like *this*."

I can picture her lying there with him, and it horrifies me. The clarity of the image is startling...her hand resting limply on his hairless chest, her smooth skin glistening with perspiration, her expression content and void of any noticeable remorse. After all, who gives a shit about marriage when you have the chance to fuck an attractive kid with rock-hard abs and a third-grade vocabulary?

Not I, said my wife in unison with the fly.

The image nearly ruins everything. I double over, dropping the knife, and put my hands on my knees, breathing deeply and trying to keep myself from vomiting. My body roils with tremors, and sweat dampens my brow. Just when I think I'm going to lose consciousness, a renewed sense of desperate longing for relief gives me a second wind. With restored resolve, I pick up the knife, stand up, and gently place one of the kid's soft white pillows over his face.

"It doesn't have to be like this. We still have a chance." She pauses, a pause full of all that remained unsaid between us for years, and then repeats, "we were meant to be *everything*."

I answer abruptly, without even the slightest consideration for the construction of my words..."No," I reply hastily, ready to get on with everything and all of it..."No, we were meant to be *nothing*." For as true as I know this is, it kills me a billion times over to admit it aloud, and it makes my skin crawl to think that I could acknowledge such a concept. The love of my life should never have been with me, should never have even *met* me...my life, her life, our lives as a unified whole have become as they are only because I made them so. I can summon so much anger, so much *hatred*, and level it at her, but it is merely displaced from myself, which is precisely where all of it belongs.

I had thought that I would hesitate, but I don't. The knife rises and falls with effortless ease while great scarlet roses blossom upon the stark white canvas of the pillow. There are tears in my eyes and a smile upon my face as I put into him everything I despise about myself and desecrate it as I was never before able. It is magical.

I'm thinking that this it, this is ecstasy, this is perfection, this is fucking *it*...and then it *really* hits me. My surroundings explode with vibrant color, the cheerful *thwuck!* sound of the knife filling my ears. Great surges of sweetly burning, sweetly soothing adrenaline urgently courses through my weeping veins. I am overcome with power, drunk on my sovereignty over this bleeding worm, stoned on his silent helplessness against the dominion of the knife, his knife, *my* knife. I am God. I am Satan. I am Man.

My arm eventually gets tired, and I take a step back to observe what I've done, panting as I bask in the warm, tanning sun of lingering residual bliss. The pillow remains over my victim's face, but it's now almost completely red and tattered to ribbons. Feathers float in the air, some of them tinged with blood. His body is still, although his feet had been kicking fitfully for a few moments towards the end. There's a large stain on the front of his boxers.

I sit down and light a trembling cigarette with sticky

crimson fingers, closing my eyes and staring vacantly ahead, anxiously chewing the inside of my cheek and thinking over and over "what now?" The smoke tastes stale and bland...at least, I *think* it's the smoke...maybe it's the air, maybe it's *life*...maybe I just have a bad taste in my mouth from inhaling too much of all three of them.

I wipe smeared blood from the face of my watch with my shirt cuff and look at its incessantly ticking hands for a long while, temporarily transfixed; there are only myself and the unflinchingly unstoppable force of passing time...everything else has vanished, become wholly irrelevant, past and future no longer applicable, and the present feels as painful as it does sublimely beautiful. I have been found, and as a result I am lost, likely forever. I should be upset, I should be afraid, but there is only a burned-out emptiness, like the drained bottle of whiskey in the other room.

I stir slightly, uneasily. The cigarette has gone out and the liquor's warmth has abandoned me, leaving me cold and alone and vulnerable in this unfamiliar place of sex and lies and death. I can feel ghosts, both alive and dead, watching me with curious, judgmental eyes as they slink about in the comforting safety of their shadows.

"You never loved me the way you should have, the way I *deserved*. You always put *it* before *me*...even with everything I gave you, it was never enough. You turned elsewhere, sought your own special brand of avoidance because you are afraid."

There's no sense in arguing with her; she's right about everything, and nothing is exaggerated. If I was ever worth anything at all, she never would have strayed. She came here for the same reason that I did…because of me, because of my faults, my failures. The illicit young lover was little more than a side effect.

While I was lost in my soundless lament, the remaining bliss…the thrill of the kill, if you will…had quietly sneaked from my body, and my environment, so briefly beautiful, had dulled to a washed-out gray hue, contrasted only by the glittering cherry-colored blood that is everywhere, that is in too many places…there's too much of it, there hadn't been that much, there just *can't* be that much blood…not in any place, not in any person, and certainly not in *him*. But it is there, all of it startlingly real, too tangibly existent to ignore. On the bed, on him, on *me*…splattered on the walls and streaked across the carpet and dotted along the ceiling. It is laughing, the whole world is laughing, and I am the joke, and there is just so much blood.

All at once the reality of my actions descends upon me like a swarm of a thousand chattering locusts, and the too-real, too-near consequences arrest me in their clarity. I want to scream, I want to run, I want to take it all back. I want it to be a dream, I want to wake up, I want my bed…I want my mother to whisper it away and sing me to sleep. I am unprepared to deal with this, I am not equipped with the necessary tools to wage this oncoming war alone, but I *am* alone…I always have been and am destined to remain so, the sureness of my fate cemented by what I have done.

And then I'm back in the bathroom, my hands under the gushing faucet, the basin of the stained porcelain sink swirling with blood. I scrub. I scrub. I scrub. I can't get it out from underneath my fingernails and I'm sobbing. I don't look in the mirror because I know who is there, and I can't bear to face her. Not after this, not after I have pardoned her every indiscretion with my own momentously sinister deed. Her infidelity has been validated, *justified*. I am more of a worthless wretch than the dead thing in the bedroom. I am nothing, and there is nothing before me, nothing within me. This is what I have chosen.

*What now? What now? WHAT NOW? What are you going to do what are you going to do what are you…*

On my way here I'd driven by a dog lying on the side of the road, legs askew, bleeding slowly from its split stomach, jerking and shivering in the spasmodic throes of impending death. Its mouth had been opening and closing desperately, its fading black eyes filled with aching, pleading vulnerability. The sight of it had affected me on a level I thought I no longer had, bringing tears of woeful grief to my strained and bloodshot eyes.

I'd thought about stopping, getting the tire iron from my trunk, and putting it out of its misery, but the thought awakened the perpetual sickness in me and nearly drove me off the road with crippling nausea. I wish now that I *had* stopped, that I *had* ended its suffering, because I would have wanted someone to do the same for me.

*That's what I'm going to do now,* I think determinedly. *I'm going to drive there now and help that dog, I'm going to kill it, I'm going to save it from that which it cannot save itself, from that which I cannot save myself.*

I want somebody to do the same for me *right now*, as a matter of fact...I am, after all, no more than a trembling, dying dog on the side of the road. Somebody, anybody...*please* end it, because I can't do it myself.

My hands are still under the faucet, pruned and raw, stingingly red in their cleanness. I withdraw them, leaving the water running, drying my hands on my jeans and then sparing another glance at my watch.

If I hurry, I can make it to the Bad Seed before last call.

The dog will have to wait.

The dog can wait.

## **Somewhere Between Screaming and Crying**

Everything is dead.

*Everything*.

The rocking chair creaks back and forth as rainwater drips from the flimsy tin awning over the stained white porch. It splashes noisily onto the warped wood, collecting in silvery pools and creeping towards Janice's bare, bony feet.

She's tearing the filters off her husband's Marlboros and smoking them one after another, making her lungs wheeze achingly and her tongue feel fuzzy and foreign, a small wet animal sleeping with tingling restlessness between her clenched jaws. It stirs slightly and she bites it, causing it to whimper and recoil and resume its uneasy slumber.

She peers out through the haze of cigarette smoke at the lawn; the scattered clumps of grass are defiantly brown and so very *not* blue, despite all those claims made by the songs and stereotypes of which fabled chicken-fried Kentucky is the unfortunate topic. So many contradictions, so many lies passed along by legions of media and subsequent mordant misunderstandings…it strikes Janice as awfully sad, just like everything else.

Because everything else is dead, even the grass, and this in particular is very, *very* sad.

Not to mention all the blood inside…that's rather

unfortunate, as well. The blood on the floor, on the kitchen counter, spattered across the cutting board, and congealed within the big Vitamix blender. There's the horribly sad image of the flesh-clogged toilet overflowing with crimson-colored water, and the garbage can stuffed past capacity with the surplus remnants of the recently-committed atrocity. Sadder still is Janice's husband, slumped against the living room wall, revolver in his pale limp hand and half his head gone, having been reduced to chunks of pink and red meat blown all over the once-white plaster, dripping slowly down to the floor and leaving sticky scarlet streaks in their wake.

 Janice leans over and vomits quietly into the purple mop bucket at her side. Once finished, she pushes her sweaty hair back from her forehead and lights another cigarette, puke-smeared tongue growing fuzzier all the while as the smoke surges greedily into her mouth and down her throat like burning, vaporous semen ejaculated from the wispy tip of some unseen apparition's bulgingly erect cock.

 Janice scowls; she never did like giving blowjobs.

 She'd always left that type of thing to Crazy Jane, because Crazy Jane is absolutely *crazy* about doing crazy things like that.

 Because Crazy Jane is one crazy bitch.

* * *

It all began, she presumes, with Pabst Blue Ribbon.

That's how she met Crazy Jane.

That's how everything started going to shit.

It was at a party a few weeks before high school graduation, and mousy little Janice had felt very uncomfortable.

She was shy and self-conscious, so sure that everyone saw her as she saw herself in the mirror...ugly, too-thin, with unusually large eyes made larger still by thick-rimmed spectacles with lenses like window panes. Her plain brown hair was tied back in a loose ponytail with a pink polka-dotted ribbon that she regretted wearing, but it was too late to take it off...if she did, everyone would notice that she'd suddenly removed it and they would know that she'd felt silly for wearing it and thus would further judge her, not only for her ugliness but also for her tragic absence of even the remotest traces of confidence.

She stood awkwardly in the corner, watching a quartet of burly football players engage in an increasingly sloppy game of beer pong and casting occasional envious glances at the leggy cheerleader making out with the painfully-gorgeous Todd Bingham, after whom she'd lusted since fifth grade. Her friends were doing shots of bourbon and tequila and apple-flavored vodka, cajoling her to join them, to no avail.

Janice was, in fact, plotting her escape when Betty

Stilworth, her AP Chemistry lab partner, appeared at her side with a sixteen-ounce can of PBR, holding it out to her and urging her to take it with glassy, adamant eyes, saying, "C'mon, Jan-baby, just drink it. Loosen up a little. You look ridiculous being the only person here who isn't drinking."

This pierced Janice's palpitating heart and made her stomach clench sickeningly. She *did* look ridiculous, and she knew it...and after all, wasn't her ultimate goal in life simply to *not* look ridiculous?

"It'll make you feel less awkward, I promise," Betty went on, as if reading Janice's mind. "Just drink it real fast, because if you sip it like a priss you aren't going to get the real effect."

After another moment of hesitant trepidation, Janice tentatively accepted the cold, perspiring can and, as she looked down on it with queasy unease, thought absurdly of Dennis Hopper huffing helium in *Blue Velvet*.

"*Chug, chug, chug,*" Betty beseeched drunkenly, swaying slightly in her heels.

Janice jumped at the report that sounded from the can when she pulled back the tab, prompting slurry snickers from Betty. Foam bubbled from the top and seeped over the sides, coating the tips of Janice's fingers with sticky, fizzing carbonation. She was distinctly aware that her face was screwed up in an expression of terror, but she could do nothing about it other than...

"Fucking *drink it*," Betty said, getting annoyed and impatient.

And so she did.

She raised the can to her lips and gulped, ignoring the stale, foul taste and resisting the overwhelming urge to cough and sputter and spit the foul liquid from her mouth. She paused only once for breath when the beer was halfway gone, and then she raised it once more and finished it with a series of large, grimacing swallows.

When it was gone, she took a deep, shuddering breath and handed the empty can back to Betty, who was grinning ear to ear. "Well?" she asked. "How do you *feel?*"

Janice would have liked to have said that she didn't feel *anything*, that this was a stupid and pointless exercise in juvenile delinquency and she wanted no further part in it…but that would have been a lie. She felt *something*…though subtle, there was a growing warmth in her chest that wasn't the slightest bit unpleasant, and she felt a slight, intriguing rush shooting up into her head. Before she had time to respond or to even fully assess the unfamiliar sensation, Betty was thrusting another beer into her hand and commanding her to repeat the same process. This time, the moment of hesitation was shorter, and by the time she'd drunk the entirety of the can, she was feeling quite good, indeed.

After that, things started happening very quickly and, one

might say, began to edge into the realm of debauched tastelessness that was nevertheless extremely well-received by her peers. The more alcohol she poured down her throat, the more confident she felt. She no longer saw herself as an ugly little geek, but instead as a lively and vibrantly attractive seductress. Somehow she ended up dancing on a table to the musical accompaniment of Dr. Dre and Snoop Dogg, first peeling off her top and then, much to the shouting delight of the males present, unclasping her brassiere and tossing it across the room to Todd Bingham, who had suddenly lost all interest in the cheerleader.

"God*damn!*" one of the guys exclaimed, wolf-whistling and yelling, "Check out the *tits* on Crazy Jane!"

Janice cupped her breasts in response to this delicious encouragement and jiggled them as the boys drooled and whooped and took pictures with their iPhones. As all of this was transpiring, she was thinking to herself, *Yes, I am Crazy Jane. Janice has checked out and Crazy Jane has checked in and she is a sexy, smoking-hot hellcat who can do absolutely fucking* anything.

And anything is precisely what she did. Or, rather, *Todd Bingham* is precisely what she did. Still topless, Crazy Jane had taken him by the hand and led him into the master bedroom and gotten on her knees and taken him in her mouth, teasing him to the brink of bursting and then stopping to kiss his neck and bite his earlobe before pushing him onto the bed and mounting him, not really feeling anything but still shrieking out a faux orgasm for his benefit as well as that of the partygoers in the other room. She wanted them all to know just how crazy Crazy Jane really was.

They really couldn't have had any idea, though.

Neither could she.

Crazy Jane was just getting started…full steam ahead, so to speak…and she had no intentions of slowing down.

Ever.


For a while, Janice and Crazy Jane got along famously. They attended parties of varying degrees of intensity and unruliness, and Jane was always the center of attention, breathing explosive vitality into every event at which she was present. The party started when she arrived and it ended when she left. She drank everyone under the table until she puked (usually on a cheerleader, much to Janice's delight), and then she drank some more. She fucked boys and made out with girls and danced naked on rooftops. She smoked pot and took Ecstasy and even snorted coke on a number of occasions. Jane, for all intents and purposes, filled in all of the vacuous blanks in Janice's life.

Until she got greedy.

In the beginning, Janice had control over Jane, summoning her at her will and using her as a social lubricant whenever the need arose. She knew just how many drinks were required to get Crazy Jane to take over the reins, and she (for the most part, anyway) was able to anticipate just how crazy things would get on any given night. But after about a year, things started to change. Jane became less and less predictable, sometimes requiring Janice to drink higher amounts of alcohol in order to trigger the transformation, while other times she would unexpectedly assume complete control after a mere few beers or a couple of shots. She was no longer always fun and well-liked, either, because she began to get sloppy and abrasive and occasionally even belligerent.

Then, at the height of this unexpected unpleasantness, the blackouts started. At first few and far between, they began to rapidly increase in frequency and duration, landing her in strange places and strange beds with strange people (men and women alike) and, a handful of times, police cruisers and jail cells. All of this eventually culminated in an unplanned pregnancy courtesy of a young, mild-mannered gas station attendant who persistently insisted on "doing the right thing", until finally he was successful in persuading her to enter the terrifying realm of wedlock.

Crazy Jane had, naturally, been viciously opposed to this idea, especially given the boy's meek and overly docile nature.

She'd begged Janice to abort the child and continue the party girl lifestyle, ever enticing despite the mounting consequences, but in the end Janice's moralistic Catholic upbringing won out over Jane's nagging pleas.

And thus began her tragic spiral into bloody oblivion.

In this sole particular instance, she really should have listened to Jane.


Roughly two months into the pregnancy, and less than twenty-four hours after the discovery of such, Janice awoke with a gasping start, skin glazed with cold, sticky sweat and her body wracked with aching tremors.

Upon finding that she was with child, Janice had resolutely sworn off drinking, much to Jane's wailing dismay. If she were to have this baby, Janice decided, she would carry it to term properly and without engaging in behavior that could compromise its health or development. Nine months was not so long, after all.

*But it is*, Jane had hissed. *You* need *me*.

Holding the pregnancy test in her hand, the little plus-sign staring up at her, Janice had dismissed Jane's contemptuous utterances and told herself that she truly did *not* need her, and that she could wait until after the completion of the pregnancy.

But that night, sitting sweating and shaking with mouth dry and eyes burning, she thought she might have been very wrong about that.

*Just one*, Jane said soothingly. *That's all, just one. You've still got about fifteen or sixteen left in that case in the fridge, and you can throw out the rest afterward. Just one, really. Just to calm our nerves. Cold turkey is dangerous for the baby...it's not like we've got a* problem, *or anything, but we* do *drink a lot, so you're experiencing some minor withdrawals, that's all. It's totally normal. But stopping altogether without giving yourself a little taste to ease the DTs is going to be a major shock to your system, and that could potentially result in a miscarriage. You don't want* that, *do you?*

If it was strange that Jane, who had been so adamantly against the pregnancy just a day prior, was now advising in the apparent interest of the baby's health, Janice didn't notice. She was already hurrying down the stairs, taking them two at a time and stumbling into the kitchen, throwing open the refrigerator and cracking open a fizzing can of PBR, sucking down its contents while Jane sighed contentedly from within her.

When Janice awoke the next morning, lathered in puke and surrounded by almost an entire case of empty beer cans, she swore to herself that that was *it*, she was *done* for the remainder of her pregnancy.

And she kept her promise.

More or less.

Jane, whom Janice now considered more of a separate entity than a mere extension of herself, was not always respectful of Janice's good-intentioned wishes.

The first night it happened was well into her second trimester, just a few weeks before her wedding, and the first time that Janice realized Jane might really be a problem that she would need to monitor closely. She had woken up from an already-unremembered nightmare, and she'd immediately known that something was…*off*. This feeling was quickly followed by the sound of slight commotion from downstairs, and Janice's immediate thought was that her house was being burglarized. So, fumbling for her glasses and then taking up an aluminum baseball bat she kept under the bed in preparation for the potentiality of such an occurrence, she tiptoed downstairs and found the kitchen light on and the cupboard doors above the sink thrown ajar. No burglar, though…just Jane, looking awful, sitting propped against the wall with a near-empty bottle of Jim Beam between her legs, head lolling and a sloppy, contented smile painted on her pale, gaunt face. She was entirely naked, breasts sagging like an old woman's, and ribs showing prominently through her taut gray skin. Her hair, once luscious and shining, was now greasy and scraggly and tangled. Her eyes burned from hollow sockets with a crazed, drunken fervor in stark contrast to her debilitated body.

"Come have a drink, baby," she slurred, holding the

bottle up in royal invitation to Janice, beckoning her to sink down to blessed oblivion. "You practically already have, anyway." A low cackle like the hissing of diseased rats escaped from her chapped lips and sent an icy chill down Janice's spine.

"I am not you," Janice whispered with shaky defiance.

Jane laughed again, louder this time, and said, "Aren't you, though? Aren't we both?"

And then she was gone, leaving Janice alone with the bottle, which still called silently to her even without the aid of its shriveled master. Resolute in her decision, however, Janice confidently strode over, picked it up, and dumped its remaining contents down the drain.

But as she did, her head buzzed pleasantly with drink and she wobbled tipsily on her feet.

*It wasn't me, though*, she assured herself. *It wasn't me.*

It happened again about a month after the wedding. Janice was torn from restless sleep by a nagging, persistent voice within her (not her own, but not Crazy Jane's, either) that urged her out of bed and to the window overlooking the back yard. Shakily putting on her glasses, she squinted out at the night and almost immediately took a sudden, frightful intake of breath.

Something was out there.

It was too dark to see much, but the pale light of the dimly glowing half-moon allowed her to catch a glimpse of movement at the edge of the forest, too big to be an animal, though whatever it was appeared to be scrambling about on all fours.

She glanced back at Dave, her husband, who was lying sprawled out in bed, his boyish face beset with a serene expression indicative of deep, contented slumber. She envied him that, for she hadn't had a good night's sleep ever since the night she'd found Jane in the kitchen...this was in part due to fear of what damage may have been inflicted upon the baby as a result of this episode, but more so it was because she couldn't stop *obsessing* over Jane's absence. As time wore on, she longed more and more for Jane's comforting words and reassuring presence, making her feel confident, and secure, and telling her everything would be all right. Her husband shared in this suffering, as Janice expressed her harried, frustrated inner loneliness by cruelly lashing out at her wholly innocent and wholesome spouse, who merely bore it resiliently and just assumed her hostility was caused by hormonal imbalances (the hormones *did* factor into the equation, but their role was far outweighed by Janice's bitter resentment at the fact that she seemed to have lost her closest friend, even if it was only for the span of nine months...the word "*only*" used in a very loose sense, for *only* nine months seemed to Janice a very irrational way of describing the torturous length of her separation from Jane).

Looking once more out the window, she again saw a white flash of some gangly creature loping along in the darkness.

She could, she figured, do the sensible thing and just go back to sleep, or at the very least wake Dave and make *him* go outside and investigate, but she had no intention of doing either of those things. It had, after all, been *she* who was jolted awake and compelled to get out of bed and look out the window, so *she* should be the one to go confront it. So instead of doing anything "sensible", she gathered her trusty softball bat from beneath the bed and once again found herself tiptoeing down the stairs late at night with a blunt weapon in hand, ready to attack some would-be burglar (although, deep inside, she knew that what was outside was no burglar), but now the hand not holding the bat was subconsciously placed protectively over the swell of her pregnant belly.

The icy chill in the air seized her veins the moment she stepped outside; she hadn't bothered with a coat, and was thus garbed only in her maternity nightgown that fluttered about her in the cold wind as the frost-bitten grass crunched softly from beneath her slippers.

"Who's out there?" she called meekly, eyes scanning the foreboding edge of the dark, sky-reaching forest. The bat had grown heavy and she now simply dragged it along unthreateningly beside her as she trudged reluctantly forward, finally coming to a stop about five yards from the thicket.

"Who's out…" she started to call again, but didn't have time to finish before something lurched out of the woods and answered her question for her.

Janice did not, at first, recognize her…or, rather, *it*, in its current state of subsistence; its flesh was mottled and greenish, its hair stringy and falling out in clumps, its limbs spindly and its wretched eyes glassy and crazed. Janice gasped at the sight of it and took a quaking step back that faltered and gave out, sending her tumbling to the cold, hard ground as the awful creature half-walked, half-crawled towards her with its baggy stained clothes reeking of shit and puke.

"Help me," it croaked, clutching at Janice's pregnancy-swollen ankles and pleading with its sick, horrible eyes. "I'm dying. You have to help me. You have to help *us*."

Hugging herself against the cold, Janice cocked her head and said, "Jane? Is that…is that *you*?"

"I'm *dying*," it repeated, and then Janice saw in its pale, sullen expression that yes, it *was* Jane, and this realization broke her heart…no matter how much trouble Jane had gotten Janice into, and even with all of the torment and misery she had caused at the end, Janice loved her nonetheless; she had brought her comfort and confidence where no one and nothing else could, and for that she was forever in her debt, in spite of everything.

Jane suddenly turned her head to the side, gagged loudly several times, and then spewed from her mouth thick bile of a deep black color, spotted with chunks of lime-green and red.

"Jesus," said Janice, tears welling up in her eyes. "Come on, let's get you inside."

Janice washed her friend off in the bathtub, gently running a sponge over her discolored skin and shampooing what little hair she had left, whispering comforting words to her as she did so. She feared her husband would awaken and find his pregnant wife sponging down a zombie-like thing in their bathroom, but the bedroom at the end of the hall remained quiet and dark.

"You know what I need," Jane said as Janice toweled her dry. "You have to give it to me or I'll die."

"I don't have any," Janice answered with genuine dismay. "All I've got is cooking wine, and the salt in that will make you sick."

"Bring it to me."

"But you'll *throw up*."

"Then bring me a bucket, too."

\* \* \*

Events like this occurred at irregular intervals throughout the remainder of the pregnancy, but regularly enough for Janice to become quite concerned about the health of the baby. She knew, of course, that she was connected to Jane, and even though she herself wasn't indulging, the fact was Jane's drinking, through some parallel or another, was having an indirect effect on her and thereby her baby.

Despite these episodes, however, the infant was born healthy and with no visible birth defects, allowing Janice to be consumed with relief as she cradled her son…named Austin, after Dave's cancer-stricken grandfather…in her weak, trembling arms.

She did not permit herself, though, to acknowledge the true reason behind that cool, sweat-glazed relief.

She told herself it was because she had a son, a perfectly healthy son miraculously unaffected by her selfish friend's reckless habit (a habit that Janice willingly enabled, but she didn't permit herself to acknowledge that, either).

She was thoroughly convinced of her good-intentioned resolution to love and nurture this child with the motherly affection she herself had been denied as a child.

She assumed with complete sincerity that she would never allow any harm to come to this child, and she was grateful to God or the universe or whatever for allowing it to come into life unhindered by the drastically damaging effects of the drink.

She did *not* let herself even *consider* the fact that the child's health gave her relief solely because it meant she wouldn't have to explain herself to anyone. After all, there inevitably would have been questions if little Austin had emerged from her as a crippled and grotesque wretch, warped and malformed by nine months of on-and-off substance abuse.

She didn't like answering questions, and by the grace of something she did not know nor understand, there arose no need for questions to be asked.

Not then, anyway.

The gore-smeared walls, the knife, the gun, the blender…that was all in the future, on a bloody afternoon more than two years away.

On that day, though, *a lot* of questions would be asked.

On that day, she would have to answer.


Things were okay for a while. Austin himself was okay, though Janice soon noticed that he had somewhat of a funny-looking face, with eyes that were a trifle too far apart and a thin-lipped mouth below a short, pug-like nose, but she attributed this simply to poor genes; her mother and father hadn't been particularly attractive people, and while Janice didn't consider herself to be beautiful by any means, Jane convinced her that she was far from ugly and had been lucky not to inherit any of her parents' worst features.

And yes, Jane was back. In secret, late at night after Dave and Austin were asleep, Janice would slink into the garage where she kept her liquor stashed in a box otherwise full of mouse traps and rat poison and various types of Raid and insect repellant. There she would sit, huddled in the corner of the cold garage, wrapped in a dirty quilt, warming herself with the fiery heat of her beloved Southern Comfort and Black Velvet. She and Jane would have long talks about the future, about plans to do great things and accomplish lofty goals, but in the morning they were forgotten and thus had to be either renewed or replaced come the darkness of late, late nightfall.

In the day she nursed the baby and halfheartedly tried to entertain him, but her thoughts were clouded and her head constantly ached. She ate potato chips, and frozen pizza, and Twinkies, causing her to gain roughly thirty or so pounds...ten of which she'd needed, twenty of which she didn't. If her husband was dissatisfied with her appearance, he didn't vocalize it, though he made love to her less often and seemed distant in his quiet, soft-spoken manner.

As Janice grew more and more unappealing to the eyes, Jane changed in the opposite fashion; her grotesque, withdrawal-induced leprosy faded into an astounding beauty that increased in splendor with each night of drunken oblivion. She was angelic and divine, a diamond-in-the-rough goddess of Kentucky white trash, so shockingly gorgeous that she could turn a man's dick to stone with a mere passing glance.

*I am the real you,* she assured Janice on a regular basis. *This is what you really look like. Be proud of who you are, love yourself deeply, know that your earthly body is nothing but a protective shell designed to hide your inner beauty, because your* **true** *body is too perfect for the lowly human race, too heavenly and divine to be beheld by the sickly eye of worm-like mankind.*

This encouragement helped greatly, but there were days where the mirror was more powerful than Jane's words, and Janice would go crying to the garage at night, hating herself and her fat, unkempt visage.

One particular night, as Janice staggered to the box of poison and withdrew her own preferred flavor, she was so consumed with self-hatred that she was unable to summon Jane. She drank and drank and drank until there was nothing left to drink, but Jane would not come. So she lay on the cold floor, muttering pleading whispers for her savior to rescue her from her inner torment.

After a long shivering time of throbbing delirium, she slipped from hazy gray half-consciousness to the sensation of a stirring restlessness deep in her loins. It was mild at first, but quickly perpetuated into a screaming feeling that she was on the verge of bursting.

And then she did.

Burst, that is.

She tore at her clothes and saw her skin shifting and bulging, until a bleeding crack opened in the flesh between her sagging breasts, widening and lengthening until it spread all the way down to her groin, spewing scarlet gore, and her arms and legs tore open and there was blood, blood, so much blood, sticky and steaming hot. There came a great rumbling from within her squirming intestines, and then a hand shot out, and then another, and then something was pulling itself out of her, covered in blood blood blood, and bits of flesh like afterbirth, its emerging head matted with long hair glued to its scalp and the back of its neck and splayed down its naked shoulders, struggling to be free until finally it was, standing there before bleeding Janice lying shredded and disemboweled in her own innards...poor sickly Janice, Janice who wanted to scream but couldn't, teeth chattering and tongue lashing, slipping out of bleary wakefulness into dark and unknown oblivious bliss for a short time before surfacing once more into shrewd reality, and the thing before her was no longer a thing, no longer covered in gore, but *Jane*, beautiful Jane with her glorious nakedness, tan and toned and flat-stomached, chest beset with perfect and perky round breasts equipped with big beautiful nipples untainted by the savagely destructive process of breastfeeding, hair flowing and shining, eyes glowing with youthful fervor, all of her beautiful, beautiful, so beautiful…and then she was down on her hands and knees in an animalistic pose, looking up at pained bleeding Janice, and suddenly her mouth was upon her mercifully still-intact vagina and her tongue lapped and the horrible pain was instantly replaced with unspeakable pleasure, and again Janice wanted desperately to scream, this time out of sheer ecstasy, but again she was unable and all she could do was writhe as Jane pleasured her with her warm fuzzy wet tongue, and when she came up for air Janice begged her not to stop, please don't stop, and a great gush of clear watery liquid sprayed from between her legs and splashed onto Jane's flawless face, and Jane laughed and went back down and drank deeply from the elixir that continued to spew from Janice's shriveled vagina, and O how Janice groaned and moaned to thine own great ubiquitous beings above or below or wherever, and her toes curled so tightly that the nails bit into the bottoms of her feet and the pleasure went on and on for gawd knows how long until at horribly long last she awoke awfully to the coldness of her bed, still warmly wet between her legs, sobbing uncontrollably and just not wanting it to be over, and her husband wakened panicky by his wife's gasping cries and trying desperately to console her, asking over and over again what was wrong, for chrissake please tell me what's wrong, but Janice couldn't tell him. She just couldn't tell him. She couldn't. She couldn't.

All of this went on for some time; the secretive drinking, the late-night sex romps with Jane, the weight fluctuations…all of this, and Dave said nor did anything because he refused to allow himself to accept the notion that his beloved betrothed, the mother of his child, had any real problem in the vein of that which she truly *did* have. He lived in constant denial, which required a fierce exercise of will that left him perpetually exhausted, which in turn aided in his ability to block everything out. He devoted most of his free time to caring for Austin, something of which Janice did shockingly little…she responded to his needs only on the most basic of levels, providing just enough motherly attention so as to prevent her from slipping into the category of neglectful.

By the time Austin was two, Dave was deep in the throes of depression. All of the joy and color had gone out of his world, and the love he felt for his wife was little more than passionless habit, for he knew not how else to feel. Their conversations were dry, short, and occurring in minimal frequency, and on the rare nights they had sex it felt forced and awkward. His affection for his son was the only thing left unchanged in his life, but his misery was so great that he was oftentimes unable to convey it in the manner he desired, which only led to further depression and self-loathing.

This ever-extending period of Dave's darkness naturally culminated in an affair. He was now working as a somewhat underpaid assistant at a consulting firm, a job that had landed in his lap through a lucky family connection. His boss's secretary, a fiery young redhead named Amanda with a penchant for discrete sexual harassment, had taken an immediate liking to Dave. He had ignored her advances for the first year and a half of his employment, until he finally let down his guard and submitted to an evening of sweaty fornication in a seedy motel room. Afterward, he'd gone home feeling different…not good, per se, but *better*. For the first time in a horribly long time, he'd *felt* something, something that was pleasurable enough to far outweigh the sickly guilt settling in the pit of his stomach.

As time went on, though, and the after-work motel meetings became more frequent, the guilt started to go away, until it was finally replaced with a not-unpleasant hollowness that filled with gleeful gratification every time he slipped under the covers with Amanda.

And so it was.

The gears were turning, the wheels set in motion.

The *fuse* had been *lit*.

Nothing like this ever ends well.

This would be no different.

It never is.

*\*\**

"He's *cheating* on you," Jane told Janice one night in the garage while they shared a cigarette and passed a bottle of malt liquor back and forth between each other.

Janice narrowed her glossy eyes and cocked her head to the side, where it remained lolling and heavy as if filled with a million marbles pushing against her throbbing skull. "No he's not," she said unconvincingly. "He *loves* me. Why would you think something like that?"

Jane shook her head and brushed a lock of perfect hair behind her perfect ear and regarded Janice with her perfect bright eyes. "I don't think, I *know*. He's been acting different. Cheating men always start acting different. Something has been *off* about him. And he's getting home late more and more often."

"He's been working late, that's all." Again, unconvincing.

"Trust me on this, honey, just as you trust me on everything else. He's fucking some floozy and he's not apt to stop. Not unless you make him."

Janice was quiet for a while, nursing the bottle and avoiding Jane's gaze, until at last she said, "How do I do that? And how do I find out for sure that he even *is* cheating on me?"

Jane shrugged. "Suck his cock on one of the nights he gets home late. You know how my juice tastes…his cock will taste similar, though I'm sure not nearly as good." She gave a little smile. "He will likely resist, as he'll know the taste and scent will be lingering there, so don't give him a choice. Do it after he goes to sleep, as a matter of fact, which he always seems to do very shortly after getting home from one of those 'late work nights'. If he's asleep, you won't even have to finish him off…just briefly put your mouth around it long enough to get a taste and he probably won't wake up."

Janice nodded slowly. "Okay, fine, I can do that. So if he *is* cheating, what then? How do I get him to stop?" Anger was creeping into her voice as she considered the possibility that her husband really *was* fucking another woman.

Jane smiled again, wider this time. "We'll cross that bridge when it presents itself."

More slow nods from Janice, and then, "This is really bumming me out. Can I play with your tits? That always cheers me up."

Without answering verbally, as no verbal answer was required, Jane promptly removed her top and unhooked her bra, letting her great globular breasts tumble free. Janice seized them at once, massaging them and sucking them and rubbing her face against their soft flesh, and immediately all thoughts of her potentially unfaithful husband were forgotten entirely.

Three nights later, Dave came home four hours late. He seemed in rather high spirits, though he unsurprisingly retired to bed shortly after preparing himself a plate of leftovers and eating silently at the kitchen table.

After having a few drinks in the garage, Janice crept upstairs and did as she was instructed.

The taste was unmistakable.

She sat on the edge of the bed for a long while, listening to Dave's rhythmic snores and not knowing how to feel but weeping silently to herself. It had been quite some time since she'd felt anything of note towards her husband, either positive or negative, so she wasn't sure why this upset her so. Perhaps, she reasoned, it was because it was an affront to her dignity, her confidence, her sense of self-worth…or, at least, what little of all of this there was. Still, no matter how low her feelings were for herself, this treacherous act of infidelity was undeniably crushing.

She went back downstairs, into the garage, and cried into Jane's shoulder. Jane held her and listened to her as no one else would nor could, stroking her hair and licking the tears from her face.

"What do we do?" Janice finally asked once the worst of the tears had subsided.

"*You,*" Jane said, "don't have to do anything. This is a job best left to me. So I must ask you, do you trust me completely?"

"Yes. More than anyone. You're all I have." A flickering thought of Austin flashed through her head, but she quickly dismissed it. The child was primarily an inconvenience and a burden, and she'd long ago forgiven herself for her lack of love towards it. She was distinctly unaware of when she had stopped loving her son, but she fancied this to be unimportant, because Jane was *all* that was important, and Austin just got in the way.

"Then let me take care of this," Jane said. "Don't you worry about a thing. Come get me tomorrow morning after Dave leaves for work, and give yourself over to me completely. After that, I'll get everything in order and do what needs to be done."

"What *are* you going to do?"

"All will reveal itself at its proper time. Tonight, I don't want you to think about any of it. Just take off your pants, lie back, and let me bring unto you the most exquisite pleasure you have ever felt in your life."

Janice again did as instructed. After all this time, she'd learned to simply listen to Jane, because Jane had all the answers.


When she came to the next night, everything had indeed been taken care of, and only fuzzy snapshots of the day's events were what remained, alongside the far more tangible wreckage of what had transpired.

As she sat up in bed, wiping dried puke from her lips, the

fragmented images began to compile themselves into a disjointed movie-like memory projected horribly on a cracked silver screen within her conscious mind. While nowhere near complete or even remotely sensible in terms of their modern definitions, there was enough for her to know what had gone on and, more importantly, what she would find downstairs.

It all went something like this:

Dave left for work just as he would any other normal morning. As soon as the front door closed behind him, Janice was down in the garage, drinking as much as she could in the shortest amount of time possible. Eventually she relinquished all control of her body and mind to Jane, and she went quietly to sleep somewhere deep within herself, letting Jane do everything for her, just as had been promised.

Static, blurred vision, stumbling up the stairs, pausing to puke, crawling into Austin's bright purple room and pulling him out of bed, dragging him down into the kitchen. Even in his extreme youth and slightly challenged mental processing power, he sensed something was wrong, squirming and crying and bleating out nonsense words as Jane laid him out on the cutting board, holding him down with one hand and retrieving the butcher knife from its place on the nearby rack with the other.

More static, red everywhere, terrible hacking noises and spraying blood, *thuck thuck thuck* and quickly the crying stopped and there was just *thuck thuck thuck* and stickiness and more puking and more *thuck*-ing until she had a sufficient amount of meat for the task at hand, no, *more* than was sufficient…she had a *surplus*, and that simply would not *do*, so she gathered up the extra bits that would be too difficult to cook and carried them dripping into the bathroom, dumping them into the toilet, flushing and flushing and flushing but they wouldn't go down so the toilet bowl was left to runneth over with chunky red water that stained its pearly white porcelain sides in grimy streaks, and Jane shook her head in frustration and stuffed some of the overflowing pieces into the garbage can and then went back to the kitchen, turning on the oven and filling Janice's largest pot with water, setting it atop the stove to boil and in the meantime jamming the gory pieces into the big blender and then switching it on, forgetting to put the top back upon it and so fleshy scarlet goop shot up onto the ceiling and she screamed angrily and slammed the top on and then watched the meaty hunks swirl around and around and around while the blood on the ceiling dripped down onto her head.  After an appropriate amount of swirling and churning, she unplugged the blender and carried it over to the stove, where she then dumped its contents into the steaming bubbles, and oh the *smell*, so she went upstairs and dabbed two tissues into Dave's cologne and stuck them far up her nostrils and then went back downstairs to finish. She stirred and stirred and added salt and sugar and seasoning and whatever else seemed appropriate until…

Stew.

Into a big round Tupperware container it went, then into the refrigerator, blood everywhere everywhere everywhere on the ceiling, on the floor, on the stove, on *her*, more static, more fuzz, and then she passed out for a while and woke back up just in time to take the stew out of the fridge and pour it into a white ceramic bowl and microwave it, and then she went upstairs and clumsily changed into clean clothes before setting the bowl of stew on the coffee table in the living room, turning on the football game, and then greeting Dave at the door, telling him dinner was ready, and that he could eat on the couch just this once, and then leading him into the living room because of course he must must must not see the kitchen, and he sat down and absently spooned the stew into his mouth with his eyes fixed on the TV, and he commented that though it smelled kind of funny it tasted *delicious*, and she could tell he really meant it, and then he asked where Austin was and Jane just lost it, collapsing into a fit of giggles on the floor and saying breathlessly I got you this time, I got you I got you I got you where it *hurts*, the only way to really really really hurt you and then more giggles giggles as a horrified look of realization crept onto Dave's greening face and a moan escaped his lips as he looked down into the bowl and yes oh fuck oh *gawd* there was a tooth, definitely a tooth, and then the moan turned into a scream that got cut off into a gurgle as red vomit started to spurt from his paling lips and he stumbled to the bathroom and when he saw what was there he screamed even louder before it all came up in a great gush of crimson bile and he puked and puked and puked and puked until there was nothing left and he just dry heaved and made awful noises that were somewhere between screaming and crying until his throat began to tear into shredded cords and he stumbled to the garage where he kept his revolver locked in a safe and he loaded it with trembling fingers as he screamed some more even though it wasn't really a scream at this point so much as just a weak crying whisper, and he came back in where Jane was still giggling on the living room floor and he pointed the gun at her while giant tears rolled down his face and he said why why why would you do this you killed him you killed our baby you killed my boy and he waved the gun at her, willing himself to pull the trigger but he just couldn't for one more moment stand all the thoughts of what was going on and what had happened so he turned it on himself and shoved the barrel into his red red mouth and pulled the trigger, splattering the wall with bloody pulp and slumping down against the stained plaster while Jane just giggled and giggled and giggled and giggled and giggled and

    No.

    Surely this had been some sort of nightmare.

    No no no.

    This had not happened.

Janice swallowed a few times, her mouth tasting of vomit, and drunkenly pulled herself out of bed.

Drunkenly staggered down the hall and half-fell down the stairs.

And there it all was.

There it was.

There it *is*.

All of it all of it all of it true fucking true so goddamn fucking true.

Awful, how tragic, really just terrible.

Things like this don't happen, shouldn't happen, and yet here it is and they do.

Janice lost consciousness. For the rest of the night, she enjoyed the last peaceful oblivion she would ever have.

And now here she finds herself in the horrible present, on the porch looking out at the rain, smoking cigarettes and periodically puking into the pail, and that's that.

Worst of all, all the liquor is gone, and with it Jane.

No one left to comfort her, no one left to take it away.

Jane had fulfilled her promise, as always, but had also left Janice to clean up the subsequent morning-after mess…as always.

But there was no cleaning this up.

Some messes just can't be made right.

That's what they don't tell you, what *it* doesn't tell you, and what Jane didn't tell her humanly counterpart.

So here is Janice, left just with a rocking chair, a bucket of puke, and half a pack of Marlboros.

And the goddamn grass still isn't blue.

## **Objects in Mirror**

"Here's the key to your room, Mr. McPleasant."

McPleasant blinked at the hotel concierge and swallowed audibly. He did not remember coming here, and he did not recognize this tall, bespectacled man who was holding a red keycard out to him.

"Where am I?" McPleasant asked, in a voice that was not quite his own. He looked over his shoulder at the lobby, which was spacious and cozy, decorated with a number of couches, armchairs, and minibars.

The concierge came around the front desk and held out his hand, which McPleasant did not shake. The peculiar man seemed unbothered by this, and he said, "Welcome, Mr. McPleasant, to the Hotel Empyrean. My name is Gressil, and I'm here to accommodate to all of our guests' wishes."

"The Hotel Empyrean?" McPleasant said, raising his eyebrows.

Gressil smiled. "Yes, the Hotel Empyrean. The owner, whom you'll meet eventually, thought about calling it Hotel California, but decided that it was a bit too gimmicky. He opted for irony, instead. He loves irony."

McPleasant nodded, not really understanding. He was confused and uncomfortable, and he didn't completely feel himself.

Then he noticed the buzzing had stopped. The buzzing that had wreaked havoc within his head all his life was completely gone. There was nothing but silence between his ears.

"Relax," Gressil said, "what you are feeling is completely normal. It takes a bit of getting used to, being here, but it's quite pleasant...forgive the pun...once you let it all sink in."

"Am I dead?"

Gressil's smile widened and he pushed his glasses farther up his nose. "Do you *feel* dead, Mr. McPleasant?"

Of this, McPleasant was unsure. He felt strange, yes, but how could he know what being dead felt like? He felt disconnected from his body, as though his mind and his soul, if he *had* a soul, had become separate entities that no longer pertained to his humanly self. "I don't know if I feel dead," he told Gressil, thinking out loud. "I don't know."

"Trust your instinct. Don't think about it too much."

McPleasant turned around and looked at the sliding glass doors which he assumed had been the way in which he had come. He couldn't see outside; he could only see his reflection, which seemed to be growing and shrinking simultaneously. "What's out there?" he asked.

"Nothing important. You don't need *out there*, anymore. Once you're here, there's no reason to leave. It's *better* here. All the best people stay at the Hotel Empyrean."

"I'm not a good person," McPleasant stated stoically.

With a grim chuckle, Gressil replied, "I never said you were, Mr. McPleasant. I said the *best* people stay here, not the *good* people. This is *paradise*, and while the 'good people,' such as the charitable, and the conservatives, and the compassionate, like to think that *they* are the ones who get paradise, they're wrong. It's the bad folks who get the fun stuff, contrary to what that Nirvana song might lead you to believe."

McPleasant turned back around to face the concierge. "The Meat Puppets did that song first," he said.

Gressil waved a dismissive hand. "Yes, well, Nirvana did it better. Speaking of which, Mr. Cobain is here, too."

"He's dead. So, I *am* dead, then."

Gressil shook his index finger back and forth. "I never said that. Death isn't something you can just attribute to any specific person, much less yourself. It's an abstract state of being, just like anything else, really. Now tell me, Mr. McPleasant, what do you like to do for fun?"

McPleasant surprised himself by smiling. "I like to kill people. Children and women, especially. And rape people, usually after I've killed them, but not always. Sometimes I eat them. Parts of them. But only sometimes." He heard himself say this, and immediately regretted it. He wasn't supposed to tell people those things. People got offended when they heard things like that. They got scared.

Gressil, however, seemed unperturbed. "Excellent," he said, "you'll fit right in with some of our guests, then. See, we pride ourselves in giving a whole new meaning to 'room service.' All you have to do is call the front desk from the phone in your room and tell me what you need. You want a young girl to murder and rape? No problem. As soon as you make that request, you'll promptly have one delivered to your door."

McPleasant bit his lip, not quite trusting what he was hearing. He didn't believe in things that were too good to be true. "This isn't real," he whispered.

Gressil frowned and narrowed his eyes. "Define *real*, Mr. McPleasant. Reality is a very thin construct that can be broken rather easily, if you know how to do it."

"I don't think I know how to do it."

Gressil's smile returned. "You're here, aren't you?"

McPleasant didn't answer, and instead went to sit down on the nearest couch. Gressil followed and seated himself in an adjacent armchair, crossing his legs and watching McPleasant closely.

"I need a cigarette, or something," McPleasant said. "This is...too much."

*"Pick your poison, baby."* This voice came from beside him and, startled, he turned to face it. Sitting next to him on the couch, which a moment ago been unoccupied save for him, was a tan young woman holding a tray of cigarettes. She was

dressed only in a short grass skirt, and she had long black hair that tumbled down past her bare shoulders. Her bright blue irises were mostly obscured by her enormously dilated pupils.

With a shaking hand, McPleasant reached out and took a pack of Marlboros. He opened it and put one in his mouth, and the girl leaned over and lit it for him.

"This is it," Gressil said, taking off his glasses and wiping them with his tie. "This is what *we* get, Sterling. Listen, you need to *relax*. How are you feeling right now?"

McPleasant took a deep drag from the cigarette and let the thick smoke waft from between his lips. He nodded slowly and said, "I feel...good. It was...strange, at first, but now it's...*good*."

Gressil folded his hands on his lap, smiling broadly. "Yes, as you should. Think about what we have going on, here. Think about how glorious it is."

McPleasant ashed his cigarette on the girl's tan leg. He half-expected her to react negatively, but she just looked at him, blinked, and grinned. "What *is* it that we have going on here?" he asked Gressil, hitting the Marlboro again.

"Everything," the concierge answered quietly. "The 'good people,' they go through life with the idea that poverty is noble and that graciousness will bring them peace, but what do they get? Nothing, Sterling, they get nothing. They stagger from one event to the next, blinded by hope and faith and fuck knows what else, and then they end up buried under a mound of dirt while the worms and the insects violate their corpses. But not us, Mr. McPleasant, not us. Indulgence is the name of our game, isn't it? *You* know what I'm talking about, don't you?" He gazed at McPleasant expectantly over the rims of his glasses.

"Yes," McPleasant replied. "Yes, I know exactly what you are talking about." He leaned his head back and closed his eyes. The paranoia, the feeling of disorientated confusion, had given way to warmth, to a sense of *belonging*. He was *here*, and it was *good*.

"We have something beautiful, here," Gressil continued. "This is enlightened paradise. This is the truth."

McPleasant felt the girl beside him gently nudge his shoulder, and he opened his eyes. She was holding out a shining red apple, her strange eyes urging him to take it. He did, and he held it in his palm, looking at it with fascination as he puffed from his cigarette. "I thought the boss didn't like gimmicks," he said, more to himself than to Gressil. He was transfixed by the fruit in his hand, the fruit that seemed far too glossy to be anything but wax or polished plastic but which McPleasant was *sure* was real.

"You're confusing *gimmick* with *tradition*, Mr. McPleasant. What you have in your hand is a kind of ritualistic icon. It's almost a…*talisman*, if you will."

McPleasant weighed the apple in his hand, running his

thumb over its smooth surface, over the reflection of his wild-eyed face that shined up at him. "Now is the part where I take a bite, I assume?"

Gressil said solemnly, "No, now is the part where you do what you feel you must. Do what you *want*, Sterling. There are no rules here. Once you figure things out, once you understand things for what they are, there is no need for rules. Rules become irrelevant. Order maintains itself through chaos."

McPleasant raised the apple to his mouth and took a large bite. He chewed thoughtfully, and then he let the morsel of fruit sit idly on his tongue as he absorbed whatever essence was emanating from it. After a few silent moments, he swallowed, and the bit of apple that slipped down his throat felt no larger than a dime. Smaller than that, even, just a mere speck of energy and sharp sweetness.

He handed the apple back to the girl, who took a bite from the other side and held it in her mouth the same way McPleasant had.

An electronic bell chimed from the other side of the lobby, and an elevator door opened. A young man in a white uniform came out, pushing a cart with an uneven lump of mass covered by a red-stained sheet. The man had greasy black hair that fell over one eye, and his face was sallow and sweaty, with his eyes hiding deep in their shadowy sockets.

"What's under that sheet?" McPleasant asked, his

heartbeat lurching with excitement.

"Someone's idea of a good time," answered Gressil with a sly smirk. "Like I said, Mr. McPleasant, we take room service to an entirely new level."

"Fuck yes, we do," the girl in the grass skirt said, setting aside the tray of cigarettes and moving closer to McPleasant. She put her arm around his neck and blew softly into his ear, making the hair on his arms and the back of his neck stand up. "In this place, it's all a cycle that never gets old. It's the same, but it's always something new. No restrictions, honey…only gratification."

McPleasant started to say something, then swallowed hard when the girl slowly ran her tongue along his jawline. "I…when…how long does this go on? How long can I stay?"

"There is no duration of time," Gressil said. "There simply is nowhere else to go. This is the last stop, Sterling. This is the peak of existence. Once you make it here, there's nowhere to go but down, and you can't even go *there* because you've made it *here*. I told you, what's on the other side of those doors doesn't matter, anymore. Tell me…do you *want* to go anywhere else, Mr. McPleasant? Do you *want* to leave?"

McPleasant shook his head, and the girl traced the tips of her fingers up the inside of his thigh.

"Nor will you ever," Gressil continued. Those doors, you see, are one-way only. New people come in, but no one ever goes out. There's simply no *reason* to go out. Everything you could ever desire is in this building. The things that happen here would befuddle even a perverse mind such as yours. You will learn things here that will alter your state of being in ways unimaginable."

"I like this," McPleasant said, putting his arm around the girl's warm shoulders. "I like this a lot." His voice sounded deeper, more harmonious and almost a bit melodic. It was the voice of a practiced hypnotist, a centuries-wise magician, a blind and white-bearded seer. It was the voice of a god.

"*Bask* in it," the girl whispered into McPleasant's ear. "Can you *feel* it? This place does that to you. Close your eyes, reflect upon your newly-acquired knowledge."

He did as he was told, and he could picture himself sinking into a gurgling puddle of gelatinous golden warmth. He let it wash up over him, seep inside of him, flow into his veins.

"What do you feel?" Gressil asked, sounding miles away and underwater.

"Everything," said McPleasant, the corners of his mouth twitching into a contented half-smile at the sound of his new voice. He opened his eyes, and the scenery had changed completely. The hotel lobby was gone, and he was now lying on his back on a huge bed. The girl lay next to him, propped up on her elbow, one hand slowly unbuttoning McPleasant's khaki shirt. Gressil was seated on a white, semicircular couch nearby.

There was a number of hallways and rooms in the suite, and six stairs that led from the bedroom area down into the lounge where Gressil was sitting. A gigantic television was built into the wall, its dead black screen staring knowingly at McPleasant. There were no windows.

McPleasant was unbothered by this abrupt change of location. Everything remained blissful. The cigarette still hung from between his lips, and there was a tall glass of scotch on the nightstand. The girl had now opened his shirt and was running her index finger up and down his stomach.

"There should be music," McPleasant said, and was immediately answered with the sound of an old song by the Pixies, a tune that McPleasant had always liked, but he'd never known its name. He knew it now, but felt no need to speak it, to think it, to retrieve it from his massive collection of newfound knowledge. The tune of the music flowed through his veins, replacing his blood with an abstract sense of rhythm and connectivity to the lyrics. He looked at the tan young girl and said, "Try this trick and spin it. Your head will collapse."

The girl smiled, shut her dilated eyes, and said, "But there's nothing in it."

"I want to hurt you," McPleasant whispered as the music droned on. "I want to please you. I want to hear you scream in pleasure. I want to hear you shriek in pain."

Smiling, her eyes still closed, the girl nodded and

whispered, "Do it, then."

McPleasant looked back up at the ceiling and took a drag from the cigarette. "Not yet," he said, pushing curls of smoke from his nose. "Listen to the song."

"Take it in," the girl agreed. "Absorb it like everything else."

Gray plumes hung over McPleasant's head, and he watched them sway and twirl to the rhythm of the music. "This feeling," he called over to Gressil, "this *bliss*...it's unbelievable. Fuck, it's good. I can sense that notion of eternity, now. I can see myself here forever. I can see an endless line of indulgence. Looking at the present, looking forward, never looking back."

"*Now* you're getting it," Gressil said, and McPleasant saw him light a joint from the corner of his eye.

"What does it take to get into this place?" McPleasant wondered aloud. "Murder? Rape? Blasphemy? I'm guilty as charged on all accounts, but which one was my golden ticket?"

"None of the above," Gressil said, kicking off his shiny black loafers and sprawling back on the couch. "You represent a very small fraction of a much larger whole. Freedom, Sterling, *true* freedom...that's what gets you in here. It's all about thinking for yourself, eschewing the roles that society tries to force you into playing. Life is one big fucking stage production. You can be a bitch in a costume, reciting meaningless lines from a worthless script, or you can be an asshole in the audience who throws shit at the faggots on stage. The assholes in the audience come here, and the actors fade into fat, wrinkled obscurity. People like you, Sterling, people like *everyone* here, are the ones who watch with a sad kind of fascination as the world lathers itself in shit and tries to tell itself that it's all for a good cause."

"How sad," McPleasant said. "How sad for the others. Oh, the things they are missing."

"Fuck the others," whispered the girl. "This isn't meant for everyone. The *others*, the actors in the play, they wouldn't know what to do with this kind of freedom. They've spent their whole lives in chains, and they *like* the chains. The chains make them feel sane. They make them feel normal. They make them feel like they belong."

McPleasant lit another cigarette, inhaled, and listened to the music. "*Where is my mind?*" he said in unison with the band. "Do I even have a mind here, or has my being just melded into one shapeless form of boundless energy?" He thought for a moment, and then said, "I feel...*royal*."

"You are," said the girl. "Royalty is just a state of mind that exists all around us."

"Trust your instinct," Gressil said for the second time since they'd met. "Don't think about it too much." After he said this, his cell phone rang, and he answered it. He muttered something that McPleasant couldn't hear, didn't *need* to hear, and then he hung up. "I have to get back to the front desk," he said, crushing out his joint in a crystal heart-shaped ashtray on the glass table in front of the couch. "We have a new guest arriving shortly. I'll be back up later to see how you're settling in. Give me a call when your new friend ceases to entertain you."

The girl giggled at this and pressed her warmth closer to McPleasant.

Gressil didn't leave in any traditional sort of way, but he didn't just vanish, either. One moment he was there, and the next time McPleasant looked over, he was gone, and this was perfectly acceptable to him.

"Are you ready?" the girl asked, placing a long knife in McPleasant's hand.

McPleasant set the knife down beside him, hit his cigarette, and said, "Almost. Not quite. Just listen to the music. Just listen."

## **Mechanical Patriots**

None of this makes any sense to me.

I remember, vaguely, naïve notions of courage, honor, valor...I remember feeling like I was a part of something that was bigger than myself, that I was a valiant guardian of peace and a beacon of hope for the subjugated individuals on the other side of the looking-glass. I remember believing that, in a society such as my own, the governing higher-ups made their decisions in the interest of their governed.

I remember this, but the *meaning* of it all is now as foreign to me as this vast, sand-swept country. These aforementioned concepts are far too abstract, too *fake*, for my drill-instructed mind to process. I'm not a hero; none of us are. We're not protectors...we're *destroyers*. We are ruthless and brainwashed drones, expendable pawns in someone else's depraved chess game.

Life's a bitch, though, and orders are orders.

I see myself standing here, now, more or less recognizing what I am, but powerless to do anything about it. This thing I've become, this murderous mechanical patriot, is as real as the rifle in my hands and the boots on my feet. My flesh and my body are no longer my own, but have instead melded with my crisp camouflage uniform.

The others don't think like this, and soon, neither will I.

Once you're here long enough, you just shrug off your former convictions like an old coat. It hasn't completely happened to me yet, but I'm getting there. Sooner or later, we all get there.

I used to think that the screams were the worst part, but they're not. For the first few weeks of doing this shit, you think that the screams are going to drive you insane. You hear them late into the night, long after all the villagers have been lined up and shot and haphazardly tossed onto a burning heap of corpses and trash. Those screams will infect your nightmares, seep into your veins, and tear your soul to bleeding tatters.

But no, the screams aren't the worst part. It's when you *stop* hearing the screams that you know your humanity, whatever may be left of it at that point, is running on empty. This begs the question…is it better to bind yourself to your pain in the interest of keeping your conscience intact, or to allow desensitization to replace that pain with unfeeling emptiness?

Once you come here and do this, however, it doesn't matter which is the better option, because the latter inevitably becomes the *only* option. In the end, it all comes down to survival, and you can't survive out here if you're burdening yourself with the weight of a troubled conscience. You have gear you need to haul around, and it's too goddamn hot to try to carry anything extra.

"Quit being so fuckin quiet, kid. Have a cigar, help yourself to a plate of roasted sandnigger. Shit, help yourself to *two* plates. You're too fuckin thin."

I look up quickly, having momentarily forgotten where I am. The others, all five of them, are watching me expectantly. They lounge in their canvas folding chairs, puffing on cigars and picking at the roasted flesh and organs on their paper plates. The fire in the center of our circle spits and crackles angrily, charring the skin of the skewered "sandnigger" that hangs over the flames. It had probably been six or seven years old, judging from its size. Keep in mind that I say "it" not out of racist disrespect (not yet, anyway), but because there's no way to tell whether it's male or female. Its face is caved in, and I can see the silver reflection of at least six separate bullets lodged in its head. What's left of the meat is starting to slide off the blackened bones and into the fire. If there had been male genitalia, someone had already eaten it.

"Don't be such a bitch," one of the other guys says, tossing his cigar into the fire and lighting a Winston. "Why the fuck would you eat a goddamn MRE if you've got fresh, warm food right in front of you?"

"Yeah," says another. "It's a little weird, at first, but after you take a few bites, you forget all about what you're eating. Plus, it's not like they're *people*, for chrissake. They're fucking *animals."*

I look off in the distance at the dark pre-dawn sky and consider this. Animals don't get down on their knees and plead in tragically broken English that you spare the lives of their loved ones. Animals don't hug their children and whisper comforting words to them in their native tongues right before the grenade detonates. Animals don't break down into hysterical sobs as they watch their family slaughtered right in front of them.

No, the animals are the ones who pull the trigger. They're the ones who urinate on the bloody carcasses of murdered civilians while chanting "USA! USA! USA!" They're the ones who pump a child's face full of lead and then dine on what's left of the body.

We're the animals, not them.

One of the guys skewers an eyeball with his fork and sticks it in his mouth. White fluid squirts from between his lips when he bites down. "Seriously, man," he says, still chewing, "you gotta get on the train, or jump off it."

This is deep, coming from a man with a sixth-grade education who's been drinking whiskey and snorting hydrocodone all night. I'm impressed.

The sergeant takes a swig of beer and drunkenly points a finger at me, his hand shaking slightly and his eyes glassed over and bloodshot. "He's right, you know," he says to me in a stupidly intoxicated voice. "Remember that shit last week? You remember that? Fuckin *bullshit*, boy. You think you're too good to join us when we're havin a good time? Is *that* what it is?"

"No, sir," I say. "Just wasn't in the mood, sir." And I hadn't been. I'd just stood outside the tent, smoking cigarettes, listening with a disgusted kind of fascination as my laughing comrades gang-raped a teenage girl they'd taken from a village we'd razed earlier that day. They'd fondled her and poked at her with their combat knives on the drive back to the camp. When they'd finished with her, one of the guys dragged her out of the tent and shot her. We left her there when we packed up and moved on, her body lying in the sand with the hot sun beating down on her dark skin.

"I'm stuffed," says the guy next to me, leaning back and rubbing his stomach. He holds his plate out to me, which still has half of a liver on it, drizzled with steak sauce and bourbon.

"Eat up, boy," the sergeant slurs. "This time, that's a fuckin *order*."

With mixed feelings of hesitation and hunger, I look down at the plate for another moment before taking it.

This is what I am, what they are, what *we* are.

Life's a bitch, though, and orders are orders.

## **Rocket Man**

"We've tried everything."

The doctor took off his glasses and looked with kind eyes at the woman sitting before his vast mahogany desk. "Oh, Mrs. Thibault, I seriously doubt *that*."

Margaret Thibault raised her eyebrows. "Why?" she asked, shifting in her seat and fiddling with the zipper on the glossy red purse that sat upon her lap. "Aversion therapy, support groups, hypnosis, detox, innumerable medications…none of it has worked. I've stood by him for years, but it's becoming intolerable. Christ, it's been more than two fucking *decades*, pardon my language. I love him, and always will, but I cannot continue to play second fiddle to alcohol for the rest of my life."

The doctor polished the lenses of his glasses with a gray silk cloth and put them back on. "Have you heard of SET, Mrs. Thibault?"

Margaret shook her head.

"This does not surprise me. Space Exposure Therapy is relatively new to the United States, and, thankfully, we of the medical community have been successful in our collaboration with NASA to prevent the mainstream media from finding out about it. It originated in Russia in 2037 and has been shown to have extremely positive results in the treatment of substance abuse patients. Basically, in simple terms, space exposure has an enormously profound effect on the mind and body, essentially rendering the abused substance in question irrelevant to the user. Sixty-four percent of patients have experienced complete recovery, and the remaining thirty-six percent displayed significant progress in the reduction of the use of the addictive substance."

"It sounds expensive."

The doctor smiled, and it occurred to Margaret that the old man's teeth were too white, too perfectly straight and aligned, to be real. "Actually, Mrs. Thibault, since the therapy is still in its experimental stage, the team behind its implementation makes selections based on physician recommendations. Those selected are not required to pay any fee. The patient must simply sign some documents, mainly in the interest of formality."

Margaret narrowed her eyes, looking at the doctor with a cruel kind of skepticism. "I don't know how my husband would feel about participating in something that is 'experimental.' I don't know how *I* feel about it, myself."

The doctor did not immediately reply. Instead, he unlocked one of his desk drawers with a long silver key and, after rummaging for a few short moments, removed an unmarked blue folder. "Look this over," he said, handing it across the desk to Margaret. "Discuss it with your husband. If you decide that you two would be open to such a possibility, give me a call and I can make the necessary arrangements for your husband's application. Based on the information you've provided me, I have little doubt that he would be eligible for selection. Is he sober now?"

Margaret took the folder but did not open it. "Yes, he just got out of detox." She paused and then asked, "Are there risks involved?"

"There are risks involved with everything, Mrs. Thibault. The risks involved with this particular therapy are described at length in the informational packet. As I said, though, the results thus far have been immensely positive."

Margaret nodded slowly. "All right," she said, standing up and shaking the doctor's hand. "Thank you for agreeing to see me on such short notice. I'll call you if Tom and I decide to give this a try."

His nose and palms pressed against the thick, airtight glass window of the shuttle, Tom looked out at the Earth with wide eyes. Despite the cabin's stabilized gravity and pressure, his equilibrium had been thrown off, and the steadily-shrinking image of his home planet did nothing to help matters. In a panging moment that was both sad and ironic, Tom realized that he had never wanted a drink more badly in his life.

"Fucking crackpot medical schemes," he muttered, walking unsteadily over to the tiny cot and sitting down. "Fifty-six years old, and they shoot me into fucking *space*, for Chrissake." Granted, he *had* agreed to it, even signed all the papers himself, but he recognized that he had been hasty and foolish. His desperation had driven him to act irrationally, making snap decisions that should have been contemplated for days, perhaps weeks, even. This, though, this had received almost no contemplation at all. He'd looked over the papers, signed some forms, and two days later, here he was.

"*Tim? How are you doing, up there?*" The voice came from the overhead speaker, belonging to some NASA peon who was probably reading a comic book and sipping a Diet Coke.

"It's *Tom*," Tom corrected, sighing and running his hands through his thinning gray hair. "My name is *Tom*, and I'm doing fine."

"*Glad to hear it, Tim,*" the voice said. "*I'm going to sever the connection, now. If you need anything, press the red button on the wall and...*"

"Yeah, I know. The red button on the wall. Got it." *I could really use a tall glass of scotch,* Tom thought. *Or maybe a bottle of Southern Comfort. Yeah, and some gin and tonic to wash it down. Fill me up, Scotty. Put it on my tab.*

"*Okay, pal, make yourself comfortable, and enjoy the ride.*"

Tom looked down at his trembling hands and thought,

*Oh, I'll* absolutely *enjoy the ride. Yessir, three days in a ten-by-ten room and not a drop of liquor in sight...that really* does *sound like a hell of a time.*

Shutting his eyes and lying down, Tom reflected that it was, at the very least, nice to be alone. The shuttle was operated entirely by an automated internal computer that would take him on a pre-charted course around the solar system and return him to Earth in exactly seventy-five hours and twenty-one minutes.

Tom looked at his watch, did some quick math in his head, and determined that it had been exactly ninety-eight hours and fifty-six minutes since his last drink.

Margaret pulled the covers over her bare breasts and watched Eric button his shirt.

"Eric?" she said, "do you think I'm beautiful?"

After zipping his jeans, Eric sat down on the side of the bed and kissed the corner of Margaret's mouth. He smiled warmly at her, tucked a lock of her dark brown hair behind her ear, and said, "Yes, Mags, of course I do. You *are* beautiful." He kissed her again, softly upon the lips, and asked, "Why would you even question that?"

Margaret looked at Eric's smooth, unlined face. She was more than twenty years his senior, and when she looked at him, she saw something wonderful and extraordinary that was, for all its tangible beauty, not going to last. She knew she was in good physical condition, especially for a woman of fifty-one, and there were women at her gym who were far younger and looked like shit. Still, age was not something she could stave off forever.

"Maggie?" Eric said, frowning, his forehead creasing with worry. "Are you okay?"

Margaret nodded. "I'm fine," she said, touching the side of Eric's hard, muscular neck. "It's just...Tom never tells me that I'm pretty. I can't remember the last time he gave me *any* sort of compliment."

Eric glanced over towards the nightstand, where lay the picture frame that Margaret turned over whenever he visited. He had never once seen the photograph within it.

"He just...doesn't have his priorities straight. He *knows* how beautiful you are, I'm sure of it. It's impossible *not* to notice you, Mags." He kissed her forehead and reached under the blanket to run his fingertips over her thigh, sending a tremor up her spine. "When I look at you, you're the only thing I see. Everything else is irrelevant. I believe with everything in me that Tom sees it, too."

Looking into Eric's eyes with a sorrowful, willful kind of determination, Margaret said, "If this space therapy thing works, if Tom gets cured, you and I will have to stop...doing *this*. I love my husband, and if there's any chance I can fix our marriage, I'm going to take it."

Eric nodded gravely. "I know," he said, and then quieter, "I know."

"But if it *doesn't* work…"

Eric smiled and put a finger to Margaret's lips. "One thing at a time, Mags. Right now, just hope for the best."

After a long pause, Margaret said, "Anymore, I don't think I even *know* what's best, so what is there to hope for?"


As Mars was slowly passing by outside the window, Tom was hugging his knees to his chest and rocking back and forth on the bed. His teeth were chattering, and his T-shirt was pasted to his skin with cold sweat. Time lulled by in a dazed stupor.

"I'm in s-space," he stammered, looking out at the vast red planet. "I'm in s-space and I'm s-sober and I want to d-die." He felt paralyzed with fear. Everything had settled in; he was in a fucking spaceship, and he'd never been farther away from a drink in his life. He'd never been farther away from *anything* in his life.

He'd never had a panic attack, but he figured this was probably something like it.

A fierce shudder wracked his frame, and he collapsed off the narrow bed onto the unflinchingly hard metal floor. He lay there for a moment, trembling and blinking up at the ceiling, and then he broke into a fit of harsh sobs. "Shit," he whimpered miserably. "Mother*fucker…goddammit…somebody please help me.*"

As he pleaded to whatever unknown entity might be listening, Tom felt disgusted with himself. He was pathetic, and he knew it. This was not the man he was supposed to be. There had been a time, long ago…*too* long ago, that *he* had been in control. He had been *Major* Tom Thibault, a confident, organized man who had his shit together, not to mention a Medal of Honor and two Purple Hearts. Those days, however, were so far behind him that they almost didn't seem real, as though they were a hazy delusion of an irrevocably insane lunatic.

*I used to be afraid of the future,* Tom had once said to Margaret when lying in bed with her, not long after their honeymoon. *But with you, there is nothing that scares me. No matter what happens, no matter what madness the world may throw at me, you're always there. I can look into the future and see you, always you, constant and unchanging. Hell or high water, widespread fires, plagues of the worst kind…none of it would matter, because you're always there. I could break and fall victim to the most mind-shattering horrors of life, but you would be there, and everything always comes back to that. You keep me real, you keep me alive. You rearrange me till I'm sane.*

That memory, briefly hanging in Tom's mind with

startling clarity, disappeared all too quickly and was replaced with a vision of a more fantastical sort. He saw himself lounging on a tropical beach, a martini in one hand and a dark, European beer in the other. In the midst of this vision, he realized that *this* was it. This was the end of the line, the last stop. He was very certain, more certain than he'd ever been about anything in his entire life, that he would die up here. The solitude that had at first been comforting was now an all-encompassing void that would whittle away his sanity long before he returned to Earth. He could not take three days of this without his dear friend Mr. Bottle to keep him company. The shuttle would land and they would find him dead on the floor, his throat filled with congealed vomit and his ribs splintered from the roiling tremors.

*Pound on the red button*, a voice within him commanded frantically. *Tell them to turn the shuttle around and take you back. Pretend that you're having a heart attack, that you're going to die if they don't turn this thing around* right fucking now!

Almost immediately, though, Tom rejected this notion. He was not the first booze-addled addict to get launched up here, and he was sure they'd heard it all before. He'd done the rehab scene, and he knew that these people wouldn't be any different than the coldly apathetic orderlies at the clinic. No, he was in this for the long haul.

He closed his eyes and waited for the maddening pain in his head to seize him from consciousness.

\* \* \*

The nagging persistence of the doorbell roused Margaret from her slumber, and she sat up in bed, rubbing her eyes groggily. The clock on the nightstand said it was a little past three in the morning, so the fact that someone was ringing her doorbell (and now hammering on the door, as well) was reason enough for concern. Eric worked the graveyard shift as a janitor at a research lab, so she knew it wasn't him.

Covering her nakedness with a bathrobe, Margaret hurried to the front door and peered through the peephole. Standing on her doorstep were two men in charcoal-colored suits with matching red ties clipped to their white shirts with shining gold tie bars. Each of them had NASA identification badges hanging around their necks, as well as identical cropped hairstyles and pencil moustaches. Their faces were grim and uneasy.

Without removing the security chain, Margaret opened the door a few inches and said to the men with a quavering voice, "What's this about? Is everything all right with Tom?"

One of the men, the shorter of the two, said "May we come in, ma'am? This is a serious matter that would best be discussed indoors, preferably with you sitting down."

With quivering hands, Margaret slid the chain off the door and beckoned the two men inside. She took a seat in Tom's leather armchair while the two NASA men sat down awkwardly on the couch. She crossed her legs, feeling uncomfortable in her state of relative undress, but the men were professional in that they kept their eyes locked with hers.

"Mrs. Thibault," the shorter man said, "My name is Ken Leroy, and this is Anthony Blake. We…have some unfortunate news that may come as a bit of a shock to you, but we must assure you that we are doing everything in our power to correct the situation."

"*What* situation?"

Blake and Leroy exchanged a nervous glance, and then Leroy said, "Everything was going smoothly, at first. Then, about six hours after launch, the computer system in your husband's shuttle malfunctioned."

Margaret blinked, folder her hands tightly on her lap, and bit down hard upon her lip. "What do you mean it *malfunctioned*?"

Another nervous glance, and this time, Blake spoke. "We are currently unaware of the cause of the glitch. All we know is that the shuttle suddenly increased significantly in its velocity, veered off course, and then disappeared from our tracking system. All attempts to establish communication have been unsuccessful."

"Are you saying…you *lost* him? How the fuck could you *lose* him? There was nothing about this in the packet. Nobody said anything about 'disappearing.' Is this some kind of sick fucking joke? Am I on camera?" She was distantly aware of tears running down her face and an edging hysteria in the tone of her voice.

"Ma'am," Blake said, "this has never happened before. We share your frustration, and we're just as confused as you are. Our tracking system covers the entire Milky Way, and since your husband's shuttle is no longer *on* the tracking system..."

Leroy threw a quick, sharp look at his partner, and Blake clamped his mouth shut.

"So...you're telling me he's not even in the same fucking *galaxy* as us?"

"Well," Leroy said tentatively, "we don't know that for sure. Our tracking system *could* be experiencing...technical difficulties, if you will, but that is highly unlikely. All of the satellites and space stations are still showing up where they're supposed to be, which means that, yes, your husband could potentially be another galaxy."

Margaret leaned forward and buried her face in her hands. "This isn't happening," she said in a muffled voice. "This *can't* be happening."

"We have a team of our best technicians working on this," Leroy went on. "And we've sent for a group of Russian space engineers, as well. They'll be arriving within the hour."

"We'll get this straightened out," Blake said in a voice that was meant to sound consoling, and Leroy gave him another sharp glance.

"What Anthony means to say is that, while we cannot make any promises, we are doing everything in our power to *try* to get this straightened out. Right now, we ask that you remain patient. We will provide you with frequent progress reports, as well as with anything you may need to maintain some semblance of comfort." He paused, and then finished by saying, "I'm legally obligated to advise you to speak with a lawyer. Once you have done so, you can refer said lawyer to our legal department, which will provide him or her with the necessary details of the scenario."

Margaret nodded and wiped at her leaking eyes with her palms.

"Are you going to be all right by yourself, or should we send for a grief counselor?" Blake asked, genuine worry in his voice.

Margaret started to say no, she did not need a fucking grief counselor, but her voice cracked and she broke into a fresh series of shoulder-hitching sobs.

*With you, there is nothing that scares me*, Tom had once said to her.

*You keep me real, you keep me alive.*

*You rearrange me till I'm sane.*

Margaret covered her mouth with the back of her hand and wept.

\*\*\*

Tom opened his eyes.

Before anything else, he noticed the glaring intensity of bright light. The lighting in the shuttle's cabin had been rather dim, but now he had to hold up a hand to shield his eyes from what seemed like...*felt* like...warm sunlight.

While he waited for his eyes to adjust, Tom stood up, leaning against the wall to steady himself. His head still throbbed, and his stomach churned with nausea, but he felt slightly better than he had before.

*Before what?* he thought to himself, finally managing to blink away the worst of the dark splotches in his vision.

This was when he noticed the gaping hole in the side of the shuttle.

What had once been an untarnished silver wall adorned with a refrigerator and a steel, built-in wardrobe was now a wide, jagged opening in the hull of the spacecraft. Coils of wires trailed from the edges of the hole, spouting golden sparks and hissing loudly. Outside, Tom could see nothing but miles of flat, empty desert terrain.

Holding his breath and taking slow, wary steps, Tom lurched forward and climbed out of the ruined shuttle.

It was warm, but not unpleasantly so. Looking up into the pale white sky, Tom counted three huge, burning red suns, each of them appearing to be at least ten times the size of the

Earth's own sun. He knelt down and took a handful of soft white sand, letting it sift slowly through his fingers. Unlike the sand to which he was accustomed, the grains of *this* particular sand did not cling to his skin, nor leave behind the dry, sandpapery feeling he'd been expecting.

He looked over his shoulder at the smoking, smoldering heap of metal that had once been his shuttle, and then looked back at the unending stretch of land before him.

"Jesus," he breathed. "Jesus fucking Christ."

For the second time in mere hours, Tom lost consciousness.


When he awoke, the day was still bright and the suns seemed not to have changed position. He looked at his watch, but it had stopped ticking. Not that it would have mattered, anyway; he seriously doubted that time pertained to this place in the same way it did to Earth.

When he sat up, he gasped sharply and went rigid. Standing before him were three figures, all cloaked in burgundy robes with hoods that veiled their faces in shadow. They were tall and lean, all three of them being about six inches taller than Tom's six-one. One of them said something to the others in a language that Tom couldn't even *hope* to understand, as it sounded like little more than a jumbled mess of clicks and groans.

"Who the hell are you?" Tom said, hastily getting to his feet and taking several steps backward. "Where am I?"

Another of the figures spoke in the strange language, and then the three of them made a noise that *could* have been laughter, if one stretched the imagination far enough.

"This is a mistake," Tom continued, taking another step back. "I'm not supposed to be here. I...I don't mean any harm." He held up his hands as a sign of peace, but the robed figures gave no sign of reaction. Tom figured they could probably understand *him* about as well as he could understand *them*.

One of the figures took a long stride towards Tom, reaching into the folds of its robe as it did so. Tom cried out and held his hands higher, expecting the red-clad thing to procure some sort of dastardly weapon. Instead, it held out a tall crystal bottle, taking another step forward and offering it to Tom. The flesh on its hand was a creamy shade of white, with the faintest tint of pale blue. It had six nail-less fingers, all abnormally long, with tips that were slightly pointed.

Tom eyed the bottle suspiciously. He normally had a rule against accepting strange drinks from hooded creatures on foreign planets, but he *was* maddeningly thirsty, as much for water as he was for alcohol. Inevitably, that thirst got the better of him, and he walked slowly towards the shrouded thing and took the bottle from it. He examined it closely, turning it over in his hands. The liquid within was thin and clear and *looked* like water, so he uncorked the bottle and took a long, gulping swallow.

Whatever it was, it wasn't water. It had absolutely no taste, and not in the way that water is without taste. No, this was something else altogether. He couldn't even feel it in his mouth, wasn't even sure he had actually swallowed *anything*, so he took another swig, longer this time.

Still, there was nothing.

And then there was *something*.

His legs turned to jelly, and he collapsed onto his back. His whole body was flooded with a giddy sense of warmth, and there was a distinct tingling deep within his chest. He smiled broadly, lying there in the sand with the suns beating down upon his face, basking in the sudden explosion of unexpected ecstasy.

"What *is* this?" he asked, but his voice was garbled and far away. He lifted his hands, heavy as his arms were, and held them close to his face. He felt quite certain that they were...*melting*...but they appeared to be intact.

*They've killed me*, he thought. *That thing, that drink...it's killed me, and I'm okay with that. I really couldn't care less.*

He wasn't sure how long he lay there, completely still, watching the world fade in and out at irregular intervals.

Eventually, he became mildly aware that he was being lifted from the ground and carried. Carried...or *floating*...he wasn't sure.

Taking a deep breath, he let himself go.

*He was standing, tall and confident and upright, on a long stretch of cobblestone road underneath a moonlit night sky. Trees loomed overhead on either side of the road. Off in the distance, there was a peculiar sound of chugging machinery.*

*Tom looked down at himself and was bemused to find that he had taken on the form of some androgynous being, nude, bone-thin, and ghostly white. He touched his face and found it to be flat and unmarked by any such human features as a nose, eyes, or mouth. Further examination revealed his ears to be noticeably absent, as well.*

*"Eyeless," Tom said, "and yet I can see." And then, "Mouthless, and yet I can speak. Earless, and yet I can hear. All of this...makes sense."*

*He began to walk, and as he did, his surroundings started to fade. After about ten paces, he was walking on empty space, blackness, surrounded only by a dark backdrop of nothing. He again looked down at himself, and this time could see nothing. He was in motion, but he could no longer see or feel his legs moving.*

*This is all right,* he thought. *I exist, and I am aware of my* existence, and that is enough. That will always be enough.

He continued to glide forward, perpetuated by some unseen, unknowable force, until the distant glow of a faraway light appeared a ways ahead of him. Immediately upon seeing this light, his blank, otherworldly body returned to him, and he could once again move of his own accord. A shimmering golden path materialized before him, leading directly to the source of the light, and Tom followed it without hesitation.

As he drew nearer, he saw that the light was emanating from an open doorway. The burning iridescence prevented him from seeing what lay on the other side of the doorway, but this did not bother him. He was certain that nothing here could harm him, that here, he was safer than he had ever been in his life.

For the first time since his pre-military days, the thought of alcohol did not cross his mind. In this place, earthly matters such as poisonously addictive beverages were a foreign, irrelevant concept.

He reached the doorway and passed through the light to find himself standing on a steel balcony within a massive, domed atrium. Dominating the huge gray room, reaching all the way up to the ceiling, was a shapeless mechanical device. It consisted of an endless labyrinth of whirring gears, snaking wires, twisted pipes, and steam-spewing engines.

A scrap of paper floated by, and Tom calmly caught it between his fingers. Written in careful lettering were the words, WELCOME, MY SON.

*Welcome to the Machine,* Tom thought, *and turned his gaze upward. The panels of the overhead dome had become thousands of small digital screens, all showing various stages of civilization and society. He saw people plagued with petty problems, stressing and worrying their lives away, all in the name of reaching an unattainable goal. He saw this, saw it reenacted time and again throughout all of history, and they never learned. They cheated, they killed, they destroyed, and for what? For answers? The answer was* here, *but they would never realize that. They would continue to carry out their menial tasks, convinced that they were doing something important, that the continuation of their existence was linked directly to the continuation of the universe. The parasitic slaves to society were content to procreate in the interest of further destruction, and thus by default, everything cancelled out. All small things contributed to a greater whole, but that greater whole meant nothing.*

*Cause and effect is a lie,* Tom thought. The eternally sought-after meaning of societal human life is without definition, is meaningless. It all has a common factor of zero. To solve it would be to erase it, and erasing it would allow the boundless energy of the universe, of Nature, to breathe a sigh of relief.

*Tom closed his eyes and took in a deep breath of the polluted air, letting the pain in his lungs serve as a caustic reminder of the diseased world from which he had originated.*

*When he opened his eyes, the Machine had disappeared and*

*been replaced by a large orb of surging yellow light. The balcony evaporated from beneath him and the unseen force returned, propelling him slowly through the air towards the brightly gleaming sphere of energy.*

*When he reached it, it absorbed him, became part of him, and he opened his eyes.*

He was lying on his back, with the ground beneath him hard and smooth. His joints ached pleasurably, and he could still feel *the drink* coursing through his veins. He propped himself up on his elbows and looked around. He was in some sort of cave, illuminated by amber sconces fixed into the rock walls. One of the hooded figures was sitting in a stone chair a few yards away, watching Tom with its long-fingered hands folded neatly on its lap.

"Are you of Earth, or the other place?" it asked in a voice that was crisply clear despite its strange, throaty tenor.

Tom sat up and leaned his back against the cave wall. "Earth," he answered, momentarily considering asking what the other place was, but then deciding that he didn't want to know. "Are you speaking English, or did that drink just allow me to understand you?"

"It allows you to understand *everything*," it said, leaning forward. "What did you see?"

Tom waited before answering, thinking about the disembodied form that had been his vessel during his otherworldly journey. "Light," he replied. "Light, and a machine. I saw...*answers*."

The shrouded thing nodded. "Yes, good. You come from a place without answers, a place with false, corrupted notions of knowledge. A place where lies assume the identity of truth."

"I know," Tom responded. "I did not know that before, but I know it now. I was blind, but that...that *drink*...it gave me sight." A question occurred to him then, and he looked around again at the cave. He and the cloaked creature were the only beings present. "Where are the other two?" he asked.

The thing leaned back and drummed its strange fingers on the arm of its chair. "Repairing your ship," it said. "You cannot stay here. You must return to your world."

Tom narrowed his eyes. "Why? Now that I have *seen* my world for what it really is, now that I *understand* it, why would I want to go back? I was *one* of them. I was a *parasite,* living off the energy of time and space but...completely oblivious to the hierarchy of the universe. I thought that I understood the way things were, but I was...*misinformed*. I abused a synthetic substance that was crafted by the same entity that I now realize would benefit from complete eradication. Human society is an ugly construct, filled with trivial conflicts and insignificant goals.

I don't want to be a part of that anymore."

The thing stood up and walked to the mouth of the cave, looking out over the sandy landscape with its hands clasped behind its back. "Then don't be a part of it," it said. "You have been witness to the truth, so use that truth to be different, to fight the status quo. Whatever you choose to do, however, *you cannot stay here*. This is a place for learning, not for living. You may be enlightened, but you are still human. Remaining in this place would drive you past the brink of sanity and send you headlong into a black abyss. Humans are not meant to experience constant, complete knowledge. To do so would be to sacrifice that which keeps you aware of your existence, and by extension of that, compromise your entire self until your mind is a gurgling puddle of nothingness."

"Shit," Tom said, massaging his temples. "When I go back, what am I supposed to say? They'll ask what happened, and my wife…" He paused. He had not thought about Margaret throughout all of this. Now that he *did* think about her, the thoughts were less than pleasant. After all, was she not just another human like all the rest of them? Blind, stupid, ignorant, and selfish? He had loved her once, yes, but that had been before *the drink*.

"You will know what to say when the time comes. As for the rest of your race, do not give up hope. You are not the only one who has seen the truth. There are others like you."

"Others have come here? Others have tasted *the drink?*"

"There is more than one path to the truth. Everything is circumstantial."

Tom started to reply, but the two other hooded figures were approaching the mouth of the cave, seeming to glide across the sand.

"You must go, now," the creature said, turning to look at Tom. "They will return you to your ship and send you on your way. Do not forget what you have learned. Forgetting is even more dangerous than knowing."


"I always assumed I would have a choice," Margaret said. "I thought that *I* would be the one who would decide whether or not we stayed together. I never considered the possibility that it would be, I don't know…out of my hands, I guess."

She was sitting with Eric at a round table on the patio of a local restaurant. Despite the presence of a wide umbrella that shaded them from the sun, she wore large dark sunglasses. She hoped he couldn't tell how much she'd been crying.

Eric reached across the table and covered Margaret's hand with his own. "We are in control of very few things in life," he said. "Most of the time, the things we *think* we control *are* out of our hands, and it's understandably jarring when we realize that it's all just a carefully constructed lie."

Margaret felt her eyes begin to sting with more tears, and she focused a large concentration of her will on preventing them from falling. "I wasn't...I wasn't prepared for..."

Eric moved his chair next to hers and put his arm around her shoulders. "You can cry," he said. "You're strong, and I know that. But you can cry."

Margaret took her sunglasses off, pressed her face into Eric's neck, and began to weep.

Eric pulled her closer and stroked her hair. The waitress had been approaching, presumably to take their orders, but she saw the situation and turned around to go help another table.

"You'll get through this," Eric whispered. "You'll get through it, and I'll be here for you for as long as you want me to be."

Margaret lifted her head, wiped her eyes with a napkin, and looked into Eric's eyes. "I'm a horrible person," she said. "I thought...I thought that I would have time to work everything out. Time to come to terms with *us*, with my feelings for you, time to sort out where I belonged and what I needed to do. But now Tom's dead, and he had no idea. He died thinking that I was his faithful, loving wife. What does that make me?"

"You don't know that he's dead," Eric said, but his voice was unconvincing. "You're not a bad person. I'm not saying that what we're doing is *right*, but he wasn't there for you, Mags.

You deserve to be loved for everything you are, to be *shown* how much you are loved, and he didn't do that for a long time. Needing affection doesn't make you a bad person."

"I still should have been honest with him. I should have ended things with him as soon as you and I started."

Eric wiped more tears from Margaret's eyes with his thumb and said, "That wouldn't have been what you wanted, Maggie. You loved him, and you still do."

Margaret wordlessly stood up and walked to the edge of the patio, looking up at the vast blue sky. After a moment, Eric joined her, standing by her side with his hand on the small of her back.

"It's hard to fathom, isn't it?" Margaret said, almost as if in a daze, watching the clouds roll lazily by. "The size of the universe? He could be anywhere out there. He could be anywhere."

She heard her cell phone ring, and she went back to the table to answer it.

His nose and palms pressed against the thick, airtight glass window of the shuttle, Tom looked out at the Earth with wide eyes. As it grew closer, becoming a huge mass that took up his entire view from the window, he thought of the yellow light that had swallowed him. He thought of the...*the drink*, and how the idea of liquor now repulsed him.

*They sent me up here to cure me*, he mused. *In a way, I guess they succeeded.*

He would tell them nothing. This much he had decided almost as soon as the cloaked figures had shot him back up into space. They would never understand. How could they? They had not tasted *the drink*, seen the things he had seen, felt the way he had felt.

They would never understand.


When the shuttle landed on the wide square of blacktop, the engines switched off and the door decompressed, swinging out and revealing a set of iron stairs leading from the cabin down to the ground. It was almost dawn, but it was dark enough that the stars still shone from above. As Tom stepped out of the cabin and onto the stairs, the cool breeze ruffling his hair, he could not help but feel a sense of longing for the sky from which he had just returned.

He saw Margaret standing between two tall men, one in a suit and the other in a lab coat. Tom wondered briefly if either of the men had been the one who'd called him "Tim." When had that even *been*, though? How long had he been gone?

As soon as his feet hit solid ground, Margaret came running to him, tears streaming down her cheeks, smiling wider than he'd seen her smile in years. She threw her arms around him, kissing his face and mouth and neck, dampening the collar of his shirt with her tears. He did not return her embrace.

"I thought you were dead," she whispered into his ear.

"So did I," Tom replied, but there was a different meaning behind his words that Margaret did not catch, that Tom didn't *expect* her to catch. She was stupid, brainwashed, narrow-minded. She was as he had been before *the drink*.

"So did I," he said again.

The space techs had wanted to ask him questions about what had happened, but Tom told them that he was tired and he just wanted to go home and get some sleep. He promised to call them in the morning, and he made it sound convincing.

On the ride home, Tom did not speak to his wife, despite her multiple attempts to engage him in conversation. She became visibly distressed at his silence, but he didn't care. She wasn't worth his time, anymore, so he simply looked out the window as they drove home. He looked at the people in their cars, the people opening their shops, the people being people and doing people things. He looked at them, and he felt *good*, because he was not one of them.  They knew nothing of the world, of the universe, of life.  They thought they were important, that they were aware of their surroundings, and that they had a purpose.

All of this, though, all of their misconceptions…it was all irrelevant, because they had not had *the drink*.

Tom smiled to himself.  He had experienced something that none of those people out there would experience, and that made him better than them.

Better than all of them.

He leaned his head back, closed his eyes, and relished in his superiority.


"He's not the same," Margaret told Eric the next day, sitting on his couch with a glass of wine in her hand.  He was by the window, smoking a cigarette and looking distraught.

"Wasn't that the whole point?" he asked.  He looked at her and, seeing the sorrow in her face, frowned.  "Maggie, I think I have a pretty good idea why you came here."  He crushed his cigarette out in a pink heart-shaped ashtray on the windowsill and came to sit next to Margaret.

Margaret looked at him, surprised, and said, "You do?"

Eric nodded and kissed her cheek.  "It worked, didn't it?

If he's not the same, doesn't that mean that the therapy did what it was supposed to do? And since it worked, you're going to stay with him. I understand that. We talked about this day, Mags...we both started this with the foreknowledge that there was a good chance it would not last forever." Margaret thought she saw a tear in his eye, but if it had been there, he hastily blinked it away. "I'm happy for you. All I ever wanted in this was for you to be happy."

Margaret smiled sadly and looked away. "That's not why I came, Eric. He...he won't even *look* at me. He won't tell me what happened when he was up there, but whatever it was, I think he blames me. I mean, why wouldn't he? I was the one who suggested the stupid SET thing, in the first place."

Eric said nothing, waiting for her to continue.

"When he stepped out of that shuttle, I was so overcome with relief and joy and *love*. I had thought he was *dead*, and to see him alive...it was like nothing I'd ever felt before. But now..."

"The feeling has passed," Eric finished for her.

It was Margaret's turn to be silent.

"What are you going to do?"

Margaret closed her eyes and shook her head, taking Eric's hand and squeezing it. "I don't know," she said. "I have a choice, now. I thought I had lost the privilege of being able to *make* that choice, of having the *opportunity* to choose, but now that I have it again, I don't know what to do with it. He won't say a fucking *word* to me, Eric!"

"Maybe he's just…in shock."

Margaret opened her eyes and looked at Eric with a mixture of wonder and contempt. "Why do you always defend him? *I'm* the one who's fucking you, Eric, not him. You've never even *met* him."

Eric lowered his gaze, looking hurt and defeated. "I…I guess I just try to give people the benefit of the doubt. I'm sleeping with the guy's *wife,* so I think it's only fair that I try to avoid slandering him. Maybe he *is* a drunken prick, but he's still your husband. I feel like I *have* to stick up for him, from time to time. I'm just a fucking *janitor*, Mags. My humanity is all I have."

Margaret was silent for a moment, and then she hugged him. "It's all any of us have," she said quietly.

Tom sat on an empty beach, looking out at the still water, sifting sand through his fingers. A gull circled in the air a few hundred feet out, occasionally diving into the ocean in futile attempts to snatch a fish.

*So simple, so uncomplicated,* Tom thought, watching the

bird. It was tireless in its efforts, despite its repeated failures. Could humans say the same for themselves? He didn't think so. They tried once, maybe twice, and then they either gave up or cheated.

He thought of the white planet, as he'd come to call it, and how *pure* it had been. No civilization, no technology, no conflict. Just the sand, the sky, and *the drink*. No, not a drink...*an elixir*. Sand. Sky. *The Elixir*. With those things, was there really any need for anything else?

The gull again dove into the water, and again came up empty.

Tom gazed up at the clear, cloudless sky and smiled. "You rearrange me till I'm sane," he told it, and wondered if the red-clad beings could hear him. He assumed the answer to this was yes, because they had *the elixir*, and with *the elixir*, you heard *everything*.

He stood up, took off his shoes and socks, and tossed them out into the water. "Good riddance," he said, grinning, and then walked off down the beach.

## **Body and Blood**

*Sunday, July 6th, 2045*
*St. Dominic Savio Cathedral*
*Villa Vida, Ohio*

The boy steps from the minivan onto the hot, coal-black asphalt of the parking lot, feeling the shadow of the enormous church looming over him. He looks up at the towering white steeples and spires that shoot high into the cloudless blue sky, and then down at the masses of people filing into the huge wooden doors propped open and welcoming to the town's devoted fellowship of devout worshipers.

He grits his teeth.

"Mommy," he says to the overweight woman wriggling her way out of the driver's seat, "I don't *wanna* go."

His mother frowns down at him as she slams shut the car door. "Don't be difficult, young man. Do you want me to tell your father about all your complaining?"

The young boy, somewhat stout himself and well on his way to adopting the family tradition of obesity, scrunches his face up in a way that makes his round face appear even rounder. "Why doesn't *Daddy* have to go?" he bleats. "How come *he* gets to stay home?"

The mother takes her child by the arm and leads him, not altogether gently, across the parking lot towards the church doors. "We've been through this, Noah," she snaps, annoyed. The relentless heat of the sun bearing down upon them and steaming up from the blacktop does nothing to improve her mood. Wiping sweat from her wide forehead with a saggy, meaty arm, she says, "Your father is a grownup, a very *busy* grownup, and he has things to do. Maybe someday when *you're* a busy grownup, you can stay home and do busy grownup things, too."

It is known to her, but thankfully not yet to her son, that her husband's "busy grownup things" consist of the heavily gluttonous consumption of cheap, shitty beer while watching his favorite football team lose every single Sunday.

"How long till I'm a grownup?" Noah asks.

"A long time."

"Like next year when I turn five?"

"No, much longer than that. And even longer until you're a *busy* grownup."

This silences the boy for the time being, and he looks as though he's contemplating this response.

A smiling deacon garbed gold and white in glittering robes greets them at the door, barring their entry and holding in his hands a large pewter bowl. "Pay your penance, please," he says with his wide, amiable grin. "For yourself and for your child, as well."

With distracted automation, the woman digs two

crumpled twenties from her purse and drops them into the bowl.

"The Lord accepts your humble restitution, and your sins of the past seven days are forgiven. Say 'hallelujah', for your Savior Jesus Christ has cleansed your soul."

"Hallelujah," the mother and son utter in unison, the boy knowing he will later be spanked if he does not comply.

The deacon makes a cross in the air with the middle and index finger of his right hand, and then steps aside to allow them passage.

When they enter the building, however, Noah says again, "I don't *wanna* go, Mommy." He struggles against her grip as she pulls him through the entry hallway towards the chapel and then adds, "It's so *boring*. I never have any fun here."

His mother's grip only tightens. "Keep your voice *down*," she hisses, practically dragging him into the chapel and sitting with him at a pew in the back. "I'm a respected member of the community and I don't want you spoiling that for me."

Jezebel is a sinner, perhaps much more so than most of her fellow churchgoers in the flock, but she is also the most regular attendee among them; every Sunday she reports to St. Dominic with religious consistency, and for eighteen years...ever since she'd been six years old...she's never missed a single mass. Her devotion is unparalleled and unmatched, and she knows it, takes *pride* in it. And pride, of course, is a sin in and of itself, but she is striding up towards the deacon, pointed heels clicking as she walks, to pay a penance that will absolve even that most recent prideful sin. If she still feels that pride after entering the chapel, as she surely will, it is no great matter because she can take comfort in the knowledge that it too shall be absolved next Sunday. It is a cycle that keeps her soul pure despite her rampant impurities along the way.

There is a man ahead of her, speaking with the deacon, the latter seeming displeased and agitated. The former is young and wholesome-looking, sporting a neat comb-over rendered shiny and hard with liberal hairspray application. He's dressed in what is no doubt his Sunday Best...wrinkled beige slacks and a blue, too-large blazer that looks as though it's fresh off the thrift store rack. His black loafers are scuffed and badly in need of a shining.

As Jezebel draws nearer, the words being spoken become clearer, and the source of the issue is revealed.

"...are *no* exceptions, sir, I do apologize," the deacon is saying. "It would not do to have impure individuals amongst us in this holy place, and you cannot be purified if you do not pay penance."

"Please, just this once," the young man pleads. "I'm...I'm

on very hard times, my rent is overdue and my car just got repossessed. I just want to hear God's word; I'm lost and need His guidance. I'll pay double next time, I swear it."

"No exceptions," the deacon repeats sternly. "Your soul is unclean, you must leave this place before you contaminate its holiness." At that, as if summoned by some invisible angel, two more deacons appear, both broad-shouldered and of burly build, dressed in black robes. They seize the man and drag him across the lawn, their faces cold and expressionless. Onlookers are watching with the quiet, hidden delight that is so typical of humans when observing a dramatic scene such as this one. Some of the old women gasp when the young man is thrown to the curb; he tries to break his fall with his hands, but both of them break viciously at the wrists when they hit the asphalt. He shrieks in pain, and then the darkly dressed deacons proceed to throw rocks at him until he scampers away, sobbing.

With this minor disturbance resolved, Jezebel struts smilingly up to the deacon, whom she knows a trifle more intimately than she should. She sees the lust in his eyes as she approaches, and she once again is filled with sinful pride, this time in the knowledge of her desirability. But she produces her penance from a purse otherwise filled with makeup and condoms, and as she drops the bill into the bowl, she feels the weight of that sin, and all the other sins of the past week, lift off her. She is clean and now within her place of worship, so everything has been righted. Her slate is clean, and she is a good person.

She takes a seat in the back, smoothing her somewhat immodestly short skirt and crossing her long, tan legs, winking at the man at the end of the row.

And so the cycle continues.


Old Gladys is what you'd call a "bible-thumper", or perhaps a bit more graphically, a "Jesus-humper". This latter is actually a trifle more fitting, for she wears a gold band around her left ring finger and tells people that she's "married to Christ". Some lonely nights she masturbates with a now-slimy and -stinking Jesus figurine.

She is the kind of woman who, at church, raises high her outstretched arms as though she were holding hands with God Himself, and she sings as loud as she can in a dire effort to drown out the voices around her. She is always the first to arrive and the last to leave so she can get in her necessary amount of prayer time within the great holy chapel. When the priest and his altar boys perform the initial steps of the Eucharistic ceremony, she whispers to herself in Latin and closes her eyes, imagining herself right there next to Christ on His crucifixion day, perhaps washing His feet with the very soap with which she washes herself, or giving Him water out of the bejeweled golden chalice from which she drinks inexpensive merlot on Wednesday nights.

Today, just as every other Sunday, she sits in the front row. She is down on her knees, praying in Hebrew loudly enough for the family seated next to her to hear, all of them rolling their eyes and whispering about her, just as everyone in Villa Vida whispers about her. The teenagers of the town have been known to call her "the Godfucker".

She knows they talk about her, and is bothered not. She knows that when Judgment Day comes...and she is *sure* that it is truly just around the corner...she will be Saved and the talkers and the eye-rollers will be damned to suffer the famines and plagues and all the other related tribulations.

She thinks then they will not roll their eyes. She thinks then they will not talk quite so much.

According to local record, St. Dominic Savio Cathedral is the largest and oldest church in Mudhoney County, but through all of its countless renovations and restorations, one would not know it and would likely doubt it if told so.

The exterior is built from materials that seem impervious to the elements, remaining pristine and untarnished by any possible force of nature. It is rumored that nameless servants climb up its angled rooftops and towers to scrub them clean of bird shit, as no such fecal matter has ever been noted by the townsfolk. Others, Old Gladys the Godfucker among them, claim that the Holy Spirit has conjured a protective bubble around the monstrous establishment.

Once inside, the churchgoer is greeted with a vast expanse of glossy marble and polished cedar, lined with 200 rows of plush pews, divided in the center by a wide walkway leading up to the altar. The seats are cushioned with soft red velvet, and the backs are fitted with squares of clear, form-molding jelly to provide maximum comfort. The floor is fashioned of aforementioned marble, and the walkway is carpeted with an embroidered rug colored a deep shade of violet. Worthy of mention is the fact that this rug never dirties, no matter how many filthy shoes tread upon it. Rumors surround this phenomenon, as well, none of which are quite interesting enough to describe here in detail.

Particularly eye-catching are the fourteen pillars, seven on each far side of the chapel, all painted to depict a respective Station of the Cross. The artist behind each of these breathtaking masterworks has remained unknown, for they have been in place for as long as any of the oldest townspeople can recall. Ridiculous whisperings of ancient, long-dead European painters are abound, each more exceedingly unbelievable than the last.

When questioned of their origin, those associated with the cathedral merely smile and shrug, saying things like, "I suppose it will always remain a mystery. Perhaps simply 'twas God who put them there."

Lastly, positioned up front is no mere pulpit of traditional structure, but instead something more resembling a high, raised stage as would be found in a theater or auditorium. Front and center of this stage lays the altar, tall and etched with ornate biblical carvings so intricate they could have been carved by elves of Tolkien lore. Farther back and slightly to the right of the altar is a huge wooden cross, sized and modeled as to resemble the infamous capital-C *Cross* as closely as possible, even spattered and streaked with dark crimson coloring for added effect. Paper doves hang overhead, held aloft by cords so fine thus rendered invisible.

None of this stage is beheld, however, by the flock of churchgoers currently seated below, for it is obscured by gold-tasseled purple curtains that, as dictated by custom, remain closed until the start of the mass.

In the priest's quarters below the chapel, a timid young altar boy sits naked on the floor and watches Father Benway prepare for mass. The boy is cold and shivering, and there is a spot of blood on the carpet beneath him.

The priest stands in the lavish bathroom, door partially ajar, staring at his aging and forlorn reflection with wounded wonderment. A neat line of cocaine...the sixth in the last hour...lies patiently waiting on the edge of the sink. He gingerly touches the wrinkled and softening flesh of his face, runs a tentative hand through his ever-thinning white hair.

"Do you think I look old?" he calls to the altar boy.

The boy is unsure of the correct answer. He *does* think the priest looks old...ancient, actually...but certainly such a response would once again bring about the dreaded dog collar. To say he looks young, however, wouldn't be believable, and a lie could mean the collar, as well.

He needn't have worried, because before he can reply, the priest answers his own question and says, "I suppose I do, don't I? Not terribly, but old all the same. It pains me to know that my days are growing shorter. I can feel it. I can feel it in my bones, and it is painful."

"I think you will live a very long time," the boy says dutifully.

Father Benway chuckles and bends over the sink to snort the line of blow with a ten dollar bill from last Sunday's collection plate. "Go now, boy," he says, sniffing loudly and rubbing his nose. "Dress yourself and go help the other children prepare the Eucharist."

\* \* \*

"Grace to you and peace from God our Father and the Lord Jesus Christ."

Thus speaks Father Benway from the altar, and his flock answers, "*And more so with you.*" Their tone is dry, deadpan, and disinterested. It is little more than a monotonous drone floating over their heads and echoing off the high walls of the chapel.

Benway, however, does not notice this. He is, as ever, enthralled by the mass of people before him over whom he has dominance. They are beneath him, and they know it so they answer to him and do not question a word he says. He is their connection to God, and only he can lead them into the Promised Land. He knows all of this, and he is high on it.

"Have mercy on us, O Lord," he continues.

"*For we are worthless worms undeserving of your love.*"

"Show us, O Lord, your mercy."

"*And grant us your salvation from our miserable, meaningless lives.*"

"And now, a reading from the Holy Gospel according to Peter." Benway clears his throat and looks over his flock, numb teeth grinding, weary old heart palpitating in the excitement of it all. The collection plate is being passed around, and this titillates him further. He launches into his reading with fervent gusto. "Two Peter, Chapter Two, Verse One…'But there were false prophets also among the people, even as there shall be false teachers among you, who privily shall bring in damnable heresies, even denying the Lord that bought them, and bring upon themselves swift destruction.'"

He clears his throat again, can't feel his mouth, feels like his words aren't coming out right, second-guessing himself but quickly dismissing doubt in contented favor of aloof confidence.

"This verse," he continues, "is critical and substantial to our very existence as Christians. When we come here each Sunday, we must remember something when we receive Eucharist; we must remember that it is *not* just about the conversion of human flesh to holy flesh, it is *not* just about re-creating the suffering of our Lord and Savior Jesus Christ, but it is *also* about the *punishment* of the false prophets among us. Be they members of non-Christian churches or mere naysaying laypersons, they *must* be brought to *justice*. So today, when you consume this sacrifice, remember this...remember what our Lord asks of us: to bring swift destruction upon the false teachers among us." His face is flushed with the exertion caused by the deliverance of such a powerful sermon. His palms are sweating, and these palms he lifts above his head, a signal for his flock to rise, and they do.

\* \* \*

Backstage, two of the eldest altar boys are standing in the shadows, passing a bottle of the priest's wine back and forth, both of them already a good ways towards drunk. Taking a large swig and handing the bottle to his companion, one of them says, "Haven't heard from Davie and the others yet...think we should go check on 'em?"

Wincing and coughing from the large gulp he has just downed, the other boy shakes his head. "No, I think they're all right. Simon told me the Eucharist is a feisty one this week, but they've got Paul with them so I'm sure they'll get everything squared away." He shakes the bottle, tips it over, and watches with a frown as a sole drop of the mahogany-colored liquid drips from its neck. "Empty," he says with sour disappointment.

"Shit," says the other boy. "I didn't mean for us to drink the whole thing. What if old Benway notices it's missing?"

The boy with the empty bottle scoffs. "That senile old loon wouldn't notice if his fuckin *cock* was missing."

The other stifles a laugh. "It probably *is*...have you heard about those priests who are going, like, full-on celibacy and cutting their schlongs off 'in the name of the Lord'? I think they're calling them 'Castros for Catholicism', or some shit."

"That's fucked-up. My parents keep pushing me to look into priesthood, but if that starts becoming the norm, you can count me outta that shit. Celibacy would be bad enough, but if I can't even get in a good wank every now and again, what's the point?" He shakes his head. "Anyway, we're gonna be on soon, so let's go get our knives. Just try to walk straight; it wouldn't look real good if we were stumbling all over the place out there."

"And now," says Benway, "this week's sacrifice comes to us from the Mudhoney County Mosque of Mohammed. Pray, brethren, that this sacrifice may be acceptable to God, the almighty Father."

*"May the Lord accept the sacrifice at your hands, for the praise and glory of His name, for our good, and the good of all His holy Church."*

"Lift up your hearts," he says.

*"We lift these evil black organs up to the Lord."*

"Let us give thanks to the Lord, our God."

*"It is right and just."*

"Holy, Holy, Holy Lord God of hosts. Heaven and earth are full of your glory. Hosanna in the highest. Damned is he who comes in the name of any who is not our Lord. Hosanna in the highest." This all comes out in a too-quick, almost jumbled manner, but no one seems to notice. Benway takes a deep breath and reminds himself that he is the holiest man in this room, in this whole goddamn *town*, and that garbling his words every now and again due to a little too much coke is perfectly excusable. With another deep breath, he says steadily, "Let the sacrifice come forth."

From the right wing of the brightly candlelit stage emerges a bearded Arabic man on all fours, bloodied, beaten, and weeping, garbed only in a filthy white turban and a scant loincloth. In tow is an altar boy of about twelve or fourteen with a nine-tailed whip in a hand that keeps lashing forward, bringing the whip's ragged ends down upon the crawling man's bleeding back, urging him forward. The boy's face is stoic and without expression.

"Witness, all of ye, the heretic brought forth," proclaims the priest. "He has spaketh against the Lord our God within his unholy place of worship, and he is of a faith that wrongfully asserts that Jesus Christ is neither the Messiah nor the son of God."

*"May his words forever scald his wicked tongue."*

Blood trickles from the wounds on the Arabic man's bare back and splashes silently to the smooth wooden floor. The altar boy continues his lashings and now begins to kick him violently in the ribs, pointing and directing him towards the huge cross.

Two more altar boys emerge from the other side of the stage, one of them pushing a tall steel stepladder, the other carrying a wooden hammer and a handful of rusty nine-inch nails.

"This man shall be made to suffer as our Lord Jesus suffered, and through this suffering and the holy blessing provided by my earthly powers, he shall become Christ upon the Cross, a victim one and the same, and he shall give up his body and pour out his blood for the forgiveness of our sins."

*"Praise be to you, O Lord, for you forgive our unforgivable sins, and we are not worthy."*

Now a procession of twelve teenage girls, all of them blonde, strikingly beautiful, and allegedly virginal, come filing out from the left side of the stage. Each of them carries a tall white candle, and they assemble in a semicircle behind the cross and begin to sing Hebrew hymns in soft elegant voices, kind faces upturned as if the Heavens themselves were just above, waiting in the rafters.

And from these dark rafters above the cross, two loops of thick black rope descend, knocking some of the paper doves on their way down and causing them to spin and swing on their unseen strings. These ropes are attached to a pulley backstage, currently being operated by the two inebriated altar boys.

The boy leading the Arab tosses aside his whip and produces from the pocket of his robes a short-bladed knife and a crude crown fashioned of barbed wire and razor blades. With the knife he saws through the Arab's turban, taking no mind of the lacerations he causes as the wrappings fall away, and then he forces the torturous crown down upon the man's already-bleeding head.

The boy who'd been pushing the ladder now comes forth and slides the Arab's arms into the two loops of rope. Once the man is securely fastened into the makeshift harness, the boy gives a tug on the one of the ropes to signal to the pulley-operators, and the Arab slowly begins to ascend into the air, stopping once he is positioned rightly before the cross.

Stoic as the others, the boy with the hammer and nails stolidly climbs up the stepladder. Once he reaches the top, the Arab, whose vision is blinded by the blood seeping into his swollen eyes, lifts his head and points his face in the boy's general direction. He whispers something unintelligible, probably a plea for mercy, but the boy tunes it out. He has heard all of it before, every Sunday, in all different languages. He is unbothered, unhearing. He selects the first nail, holding the rest of them between his teeth, and begins his work.

The hammer-blows echo throughout the cathedral, pointedly resolute in their resounding thunder.


The Godfucker's eyes are open.

Gladys usually closes her eyes during the actual crucifixion, not out of revulsion, but simply so she can envision herself at the site of *the* Crucifixion. Today, however, she is watching the ceremony with eager attentiveness.

She is particularly pleased with this week's sacrifice; last week's had been disappointing…a mottled, Satan-worshipping young junkie who had seemed too strung out to care about what was happening to him. It had been a lackluster mass, and she'd left with a bad taste in her mouth.

This week, though, is different. She does not consider herself racist by any means whatsoever, but she knows about those dirty Muslims, and she knows that they all need to be put to death. Filthy, stinking animals they are…of this she is certain because she's seen it on the Television, how they blow themselves up and beat their numerous wives and eat their own feces. She read somewhere that their preferred method of copulation is anal sodomy, the thought of which makes Gladys sick to her stomach. Her blue-haired bingo-buddy also informed her that they achieve erotic stimulation through the act of urinating and defecating on each other, and that it has been scientifically proven that they descended from prehistoric tapeworms.

So yes, she thinks Father Benway did a fine job of selecting the sacrifice this week.

Gladys's smile continues to widen in appropriation with the Arab's loudening screams.

*　*　*

Jezebel is only paying partial attention to the ceremony. At the moment, she's eyeing the altar boy who is pounding the nails into the Eucharist, wondering how much money she could squeeze out of him. He looks to be about fourteen or fifteen, and with the right approach, she supposes she could get him to raid Daddy's wallet or Mommy's purse without much reservation.

She has no qualms or reservations about engaging such young clients; they're easy targets and the duration of their stamina is significantly less than their older counterparts, so she can be done with them quickly. She charges not per hour but instead per ejaculation, which works out quite nicely with the young ones because some of them are done as soon as she takes off her top.

Her ruminations are interrupted when an infant a few rows ahead of her begins to wail. She clenches her fists and bites the inside of her cheek…the only thing she hates more than a baby is a *crying* baby, and she believes that severe corporal punishment should be issued when an infant cries in public…to both the mother *and* the child. She herself has had eleven abortions, thankfully always before the little brat inside her has time to affect her figure.

Granted, she is aware that her frequent trips to the abortion clinic (she even has a discount card that gets her half price on every third terminated pregnancy) would be frowned upon by the Catholic community, but she justifies it with the contention that in the end she's doing society a favor. The media keeps talking about the increasingly problematic population growth, so Jezebel's theory is this: The world can't afford it, so just fucking abort it. She'd had that put on a bumper sticker a few years back and slapped it on her little red Honda Accord, but after she got her tires slashed for the fourth time, she begrudgingly covered it up with one that simply says "God Bless America."

Alas, the woman with the shrieking baby chose not to abide by Jezebel's words of wisdom, so the piercing cries carry on. It's okay, though, because now the Arab's screams are increasing in volume as the altar boy pounds nails into his feet, and this drowns out the unhappy infant. This is good. Jezebel would take a screaming crucified Arab over a crying baby any day of the week.

Especially Sunday.


Little Noah is fidgeting.

He hates sitting still for long periods of time, and hates even more sitting still for things that bore him, such as Sunday mass. He looks over at his mother, who is watching the action on stage with a distracted kind of half-interest...unbeknownst to him, she is thinking about what she needs to get at the grocery store later, as well as debating on whether or not she's going to let her slob of a husband fuck her tonight.

    To Noah's right is a frail old man, his eyes shut and his chin resting on his chest, soft snores emitting from his enormous nose. There are tufts of white hair growing out of his ears, and this bothers Noah, so he turns around to look at the black family behind him. All of them are completely absorbed in the crucifixion, save for a young girl about Noah's age. This girl is the only member of the family who notices Noah's staring observation of them, and she returns his gaze with a blank stare of her own. She has tangled, knotted pigtails on either side of her head, and the whites of her eyes have a somewhat yellow glaze over them. Noah is suddenly terrified of this girl, though he doesn't know why, so he quickly turns back around to face forward.

    For several achingly long minutes, he tries to pay attention to what's happening on the stage, but this proves to be unbearably boring; the Arab's suffering means nothing to him…he sees far more interesting acts of extreme violence on his favorite Saturday morning cartoons. Yesterday he laughed hysterically as Mickey Mouse tore open Minnie Mouse's red and white polka-dotted dress and then proceeded to savagely rape her before bashing her face into a bloody pink mess with a wooden mallet much like the one being used to pound nails into the man up on the cross right now. An unfamiliar phenomenon had occurred then, too, when Noah's tiny penis began to stiffen as he watched the carnal savagery unfold on the glowing screen. This had confused him, because never before had he experienced this peculiar hardening and enlargement in his beloved genital area, but it had not been unpleasant, so he just kept watching the program, albeit with significantly increased interest.

*This*, however, fails to captivate Noah. It's the same thing every week…some guy or gal getting whipped and beaten and nailed to the cross and whatnot…the unchanging repetition of it annoys Noah. He'd love to see some chainsaws or bazookas get thrown into the mix, or perhaps see Daffy Duck come prancing onto the stage wielding his signature meat cleaver and power drill.

Of course, none of these things can be expected to occur, so Noah resorts to chewing on the cover of the hymnal, simply because this seems like the only thing to do at the moment.

With the bleeding, weeping Arab now effectively nailed in place, the choir of girls, still singing, always singing, comes to stand at the front of the stage, six on either side of the pulpit, their candles continuing to flicker and burn, casting a haunting glow upon their ghostly faces.

Father Benway steps down from the podium and strides elegantly over to the cross, standing before it and looking up at the man upon it. He raises both hands, palms facing the Arab, and says, "With my blessing and the earthly powers vested in me, you shall become Jesus incarnated upon the Cross, in mimicry of the torture inflicted upon Him. Your body and blood is now forfeit for the forgiveness of our sins, and I anoint you in the name of the Father, the Son, and the Holy Spirit."

"*Amen,*" the audience says.

More altar boys are marching onto the stage, two of them stumbling a little, all carrying a shining silver platter in one hand and a long serrated knife in the other. The first boy in line ascends the ladder and, without any hesitation, begins cutting small slices of flesh from the Arab's torso and placing them neatly on the platter. Once his plate is full, he climbs back down, drops his knife at the foot of the cross, and then goes to stand behind the line of singing girls while another boy repeats this process.

Once all of the altar boys have filled their respective platters with little slabs of bloody flesh, one last boy emerges from behind the curtains, carrying a huge silver pitcher and a long curved knife. He is young and timid and small, the very boy who'd been Father Benway's bedchamber company this morning. He walks oddly, looking almost as if the movement is causing him pain.

He ascends the ladder, pausing at the top to look with wide eyes at the man before him; he is no longer screaming or crying, but is instead just breathing raggedly, head lolled to one side, blood seeping and squirting from the hundreds of wounds on his body. There are flecks of spittle and gore in his dense beard, and thick strings of bloody snot are dripping from his wide nostrils. He does not so much as look at the boy.

"This is my first time doing this," whispers the boy meekly. "They tell me this is what God wants, but I'm not so sure. If it isn't, please ask Him to forgive me." At this last, after one final moment of hesitation, he slashes the Arab's throat.

The blood shoots out in rivers and freshets, and the boy hurriedly holds the pitcher beneath the man's neck until it is full. Then, glancing once more at the choking, sputtering man dying upon the cross, he carefully walks back down the ladder and goes to join the other boys.

They break off into two groups, walking single-file to either side of the stage, descending the steps onto the floor, and then coming to stand in line before the rows upon rows of filled pews, a few yards away from the end of the long purple rug down the center. The boy with the pitcher of blood stands front and center, willing his hands to stop shaking. It would not do to drop the blood of Christ. It would not do at all.

From his place above, the priest gestures with both hands to the boys holding the platters and says to his flock, "And so

Jesus said, 'Take this, all of you, and eat it, for this is my body which will be given up for you.'" He then gestures to the boy with the pitcher and continues, "Take this, all of you, and drink from it, for this is the chalice of my blood, the blood of the new and everlasting covenant, which will be poured out for you and for many for the forgiveness of sins. Do this in memory of me.'"

The people come, row by row, starting at the front and moving back. Each person takes a slab of dark flesh from one of the platters and places it in his or her mouth, chewing absently as one would chew any other source of ordinary nourishment, and then washing it down with a small sip of blood from the pitcher before returning to his or her seat to commence post-communion prayer. It is a long process, usually taking upwards of half an hour for everyone to receive communion, but wondrously, there is never a shortage of flesh or blood. It is generally accepted that this is due to careful calculations of the church's maximum capacity, requiring each of the boys to cut an exact amount of meat slivers to ensure that all the churchgoers are fed, and that the size of the pitcher is designed in accordance with the church's capacity, as well. Others, though, insist that it is only through the Lord's magic that no churchgoer is ever denied communion due to a lack of sufficient resources.

With the Eucharist distributed and the sacrifice hanging still and dead upon the bloodstained cross, the mass is all but concluded. The choir girls are the first to exit, singing, of course,

"Ave Maria" as they leave the stage. Then go the altar boys, silent and stern-faced, their bloodstained plates balanced in their palms.

Standing at his pulpit, the early symptoms of a coke crash beginning to set in, the sweating priest addresses his crowd. "Go now, and may the Lord be with you in all things. Sin if it is necessary, so long as you are committed to return here next Sunday to have any such sins absolved. Let us now lastly proclaim the order of our three priorities."

*"First our church, then our God, then our useless and wretched lives."*

"Amen, you are dismissed."

Upon this dismissal, the church erupts into a chorus of chatter as the churchgoers begin to file out towards the exit, milling slowly like cattle, talking and gossiping and laughing. The man on the cross is forgotten as soon as their backs are turned against him, and all are relieved to be released into another week of sinful debauchery that they know will be forgiven with next week's deposit of penance.

The curtains close.

*Exeunt*, and amen.

## **Coming Down**

The town of Millhaven lies to the east of and adjacent to its neighboring cities Villa Vista and Villa Vida, the former mainly being a bustling shopping district brimming with strip malls and superstores, and the latter entirely being a socialite cesspool of suburban corruption. The Villas are both known for their concentration of uppity yuppie communities and snobbish decadence, whereas Millhaven is of decidedly less repute and esteem than its sister cities; the buildings are older, the denizens poorer, the neighborhoods seedier and the scenery blander. While by no means a ghetto or slum, it is by and large the ugly duckling of Mudhoney County, made even more so by its unfortunately close proximity to the much more opulent Villas.

Millhaven's only feature of any real note (one prided by the locals but looked down upon by those hailing from other parts of the county, the Villas in particular) is Jubilee Street, a long, dimly-lit stretch of road cratered by potholes and crammed with dive bars, shady nightclubs, head shops, pawn shops, chop shops, and cheap strip joints. A jagged scar slicing through the center of what is otherwise a decent-enough small town of dully ordinary plainness, Jubilee Street is regarded as a kind of Sodom and Gomorra of Mudhoney, a place to which outwardly-upstanding churchgoers and restless husbands in the throes of midlife crises secretly flock for their required doses of neon-lit sin and drunken debauchery.

Perched atop a high hill overlooking Jubilee Street like a disapproving parent is the Church of the Holy Redeemer, a small white chapel dating back to the mid-nineteenth century with a vast but poorly-tended cemetery directly behind it. Otherwise indiscriminate, it was at this very hilltop cemetery, on a Saturday in 2057, that the risen Jesus Christ made his (no capital *H*, for reasons later to be divulged) first appearance.

It was a grim morning, with low-hanging charcoal clouds coughing out great windy torrents of chilly gray rain. Larry Lazlo, aged twenty-four at the time of his recent heroin-induced demise, lay enclosed within a glossy cedar casket, rainwater sliding off its sides as it was lowered into the newly-dug grave encircled by black-clad mourners standing soberly beneath their dripping umbrellas. The parents of the deceased wept silent tears as the priest spoke stoically of ashes and dust. If anyone noticed the out-of-place stranger, tall and pale and stern-faced with feet attired in cowboy boots the color of burnt brimstone, they made no mention of it.

They *did*, however, notice the man who was slowly ascending the hill, garbed lavishly in flowing white robes and sporting long, wavy brown hair and a thick red beard offset by soft, pale-blue eyes. There were large, badly-healed holes in his palms and feet. He carried no umbrella and was thus soaked to the bone, but he showed no apparent qualm with this.

"Wipe away your mournful tears, my children," the bearded man said as he came upon the gathered group. "This young man is not lost, for Death shall not claim him this day."

The priest had stopped reading, and all eyes were now fixed on this unwelcome newcomer, whom several of the group had concluded must be a stray vagrant with a booze-addled brain and an inexcusable lack of respect for this exclusively private ceremony.

"Behold, all of you," the man continued, "I stand before you as the Earthly body of your Lord and Savior Jesus Christ, risen once more to lead the faithful to the Promised Land. Observe now as I return life unto young Lawrence Lazlo, taken so tragically before his time."

Angry whisperings among the crowd had begun to circulate, with a number of the male mourners conferring with each other in regards to the potential (and forceful, inevitably) removal of the surprise guest, for lack of a better term.

The man claiming to be Christ came forth and stood before the dark rectangle of the new grave, holding his holey hands out and looking slightly upward into the stormy gray clouds. A splintered bolt of white-blue lightning streaked across the sky and brightly illuminated Christ's face, wet with rain and flushed from the damp cold.

"Lawrence Lazlo," Jesus began, "son of Harold Lazlo and Juliet Beecher-Lazlo, may you now *RISE* from your wooden tomb and beset these mourners with the purest joy at your return. I command this in the name of God the Father, ruler of Heaven and Earth!"

Everyone was dead silent, eyes shifting from the robed man to the coffin and then back to the man. The coffin remained sealed tightly shut, unmoved, with no signs of restored life from within.

Jesus looked down into the grave at the still and silent coffin, a flicker of nervous doubt flashing across his bearded face. He cleared his throat and raised his hands higher over his head, exclaiming loudly, *"LAWRENCE LAZLO, I COMMAND THEE TO COME DOWN FROM THE HEAVENS AND RETURN TO YOUR EARTHLY BODY, IN THE NAME OF THE LORD!"*

Nothing.

Jesus, now looking most uncomfortable and perhaps even somewhat embarrassed, cleared his throat again and was about to commence another increasingly futile command when two men...Larry's father and uncle, both of them tall and of not inconsiderable weight...seized him by the arms and dragged him away from the black circle of distraught mourners. Before he could utter a word in his defense, his stomach and face were blasted with a flurry of hard fists as the two men struck at him again and again, until he was knocked off his feet and sent tumbling backward, rolling down the steep muddy hill. His head caught the blunt edge of a large rock towards the bottom of the hill, sending a flash of searing white pain into his skull before the world around him went ever grayer and he shut his eyes and let numbed unconsciousness claim him, no longer feeling the rain on his face as he lay there bruised and bleeding in the soft, slushy wet grass.

Atop the hill, still unnoticed by the others, the pale man smiled darkly.

When Jesus awoke, the rainclouds had parted and given way to a clear blue sky with bright, early-afternoon sunshine that beat pleasantly down upon him and warmed his bloodied face. He sat up, his head throbbing and spinning, and looked around dazedly. The morning's events flooded back to him in a rush of pained and confused images, and he was filled with renewed dismay at his failed attempt at a miraculous display of holy prowess.

*It's been a while,* he told himself silently as he got shakily to his feet, his sandals slipping slightly in the mostly-dried mud. *I'm just rusty, that's all. Resurrection is probably too big a task with which to begin. I'll start off with something smaller and then go from there. Nothing to worry about.*

Once out of the mud, he got to his knees and said a quick prayer to his father, asking for strength, and then got back up and looked around, trying to decide where to go next. To his left lay dreary and downtrodden Jubilee Street, but he knew all too well what sin dwelt there, and he figured that it wasn't the best place to begin his search for devout followers to be ushered into the Promised Land before the initiation of Rapture, so he headed off in the other direction towards the town square.

He received raised-eyebrow sideways glances from passersby, but other than that he was paid little attention. He was aware that his appearance left something to be desired…mud-caked robes, bruised face smeared with dried blood, hands and feet pierced with gaping holes…but no matter, for soon all would be witness to his divine might, and the faithful would flock to him, and praise him and fall to their knees to kiss his muddy feet.

After passing the town municipal center and the neighboring fire department, Jesus spotted something that was perfectly suited to his current needs…a large stone fountain, with crystal clear water shooting high into the air and falling back down into a wide round basin filled with the glittering coins of the wishful. A few mothers stood scattered around it with their children, smilingly tossing pennies into the shimmering water.

Jesus smiled, for he knew this would be an easy task.

He came forward and stood upon the edge of the fountain, raising his arms over his head proclaiming, "Hear ye good people of Millhaven, I am your Lord and Savior Jesus Christ, returned to Earth to gather those who rightfully claim me."

The mothers nervously pulled their children away from the fountain, regarding Jesus with apprehensive expressions. Groups of pedestrians stopped to watch this surely-crazed man, keeping safe distance lest he be a dangerous escapee from the somewhat nearby Anson Asylum.

"Observe, all of you, and quake with wonder as I use my heavenly powers to turn this water into wine!" Jesus cried, and then promptly stepped down into the fountain's basin, almost slipping on the carpet of coins. He fell to his knees, plunged his holed hands into the water, and shouted to the sky, "O Lord, Heavenly Father full of glory, give unto me the power to turn this water to wine!"

A hushed silence came over the onlookers as…

Nothing happened.

Jesus stood up, frowning, and waved his hands over the water. "Obey my command, O water, and turn thyself to wine!"

Still nothing. The observers began to walk away, casting anxious glances back at what they perceived to be no more than a raving lunatic, likely under the influence of powerful hallucinogens.

"SUBMIT TO MY HEAVENLY MIGHT!" Jesus bellowed, kicking and splashing angrily about in the water as any remaining stragglers hurried away. The water remained unchanged.

Defeated, Jesus sat down miserably in the water and buried his face in his wet hands. "My God," he whimpered quietly, "why hast thou forsaken me?"

He walked off aimlessly down the sidewalk, ignoring gawking glances from the perplexed drivers of the cars that trundled along the poorly-maintained road. Now sopping wet in addition to his prior-attained attributes of unkempt disarray, he looked more like a homeless wretch than ever.

He kept his head down, deep in thought, pondering what could possibly be the problem. His head throbbed painfully with frustrated concentration, and his every step was punctuated by the sickly squishing noise of his feet pressing into his soaked sandals. The sun was beginning to set on the purple dusk horizon over Jubilee Street, thus offering little warmth with which to dry his dripping robes. His long wet hair felt cold against his neck, and it was beginning to take on somewhat of a frizzy quality as the moisture slowly evaporated from the knotted tangles of the mane that had been luscious and sleek just that morning.

As he trudged sullenly forward, head hanging low, he

nearly bumped into an old man and stepped aside just in time to narrowly avoid a collision. The man walked with a slow, hunched gait, with a long white cane waving back and forth in front of him like some cautionary metronome. His liver-spotted skull was capped with a crown of slicked-back platinum hair, his face grizzled with patchy white stubble. Perched over his eyes was a pair of enormous black sunglasses that caught the sly glint of the setting sun upon their lenses and reflected it back at Jesus' wounded face.

"Watch where yer goin, kid," the old man grunted. "Just 'cause I can't see you don't mean I don't know you just about ran me down there."

Jesus did not at first reply, for he was silently thanking God for what he was sure was a sign from the Heavens; certainly this man had been placed in his path so that he could restore his sight and thereby prove his holiness. After all, it *was* quite perfect, wasn't it? Making the blind man see? It was so classic it bordered on cliché, but Jesus knew all of beggars and their inability to choose, so he said to the blind man, "Hear me, blind man, for I am your Lord and Savior Jesus Christ, and I shall now bestow unto you the gift of restored sight!"

The blind man regarded him with a long, drooping frown. "You tryin to be fuckin funny, punk? You think it's funny to make fun of old blind men?"

Jesus raised his hands and inclined his head towards the

sky, ignoring the man's accusatory inquiry. "Father," he said in his mightiest voice, "I ask that you give me the power to grant this man sight, so that he may once again behold the beauty that is life and all of the tangible gifts you have so graciously set upon this world!" He waited a moment, and when he was reasonably confident that he had the power which he had requested, he pointed his fingertips at the blind man and cried, "Blind man, I command thee to *SEE!*"

The old man stood there, face darkening and frown lengthening, and then a low, guttural growl emitted from his pale lips. With speed and deftness surprising for a man of his advanced age, he thrust his cane forward and jabbed it into Christ's stomach, causing him to double over and blurt out a coughing, gasping moan. Without giving him time to recover, the man then swung the cane in a whistling arc that struck Jesus on the side of his face, hard enough to break the skin and draw blood. Almost as if in continuance of the same motion, the cane curved downward and cracked against Jesus' leg, sending him down to his knees. He clapped a hand to his bleeding face, blood running through the hole in his palm, and then the blind man delivered a final blow to his rib cage. Jesus felt something in his chest crack, and he collapsed onto his side, wheezing and weeping.

"That oughta teach you a little respect, you sick prick," the old man said venomously before spitting a great green glob of phlegmy mucus onto Christ's blood-and-mud-spattered face. "Just 'cause I can't see don't mean I don't know how to whup some ignorant little punk's ass. Now go fuck yerself, kid." He stood a moment longer over his defeated victim, and then he turned and continued along his way, cane swinging innocently back and forth in front of him as if its violent secondary purpose had been completely forgotten.

Jesus rolled over onto his back and looked up at the ever-darkening sky. "My Lord," he said, "I have failed you."

There then came the sudden sound of slow, leisurely footsteps drawing near, and a long and lanky shadow fell over him. A voice, presumably belonging to the owner of the aforementioned footsteps and shadow, said in a sticky smooth tone, "That, my friend, is where you are mistaken. You have failed no one. On the contrary, *God* has failed *you*."

Jesus propped himself up on his elbow and squinted up at the figure above him. He was lean and handsome, with stylishly tousled dark hair and a pale, elegant face rendered slightly rugged by stubbly facial hair. His eyes were a molten black, just a shade or two lighter than his pinprick pupils, and the teeth revealed in his snarky, shark-like grin were bright and sparkling, aligned in rows so perfect that even the best of oral surgeons couldn't possibly hope to replicate. His trim figure was adorned with the most extravagant of attire; his long legs were clad in torn Dusault jeans, his feet in shining pointed cowboy boots, and he wore a pinstriped Armani sport jacket over a white silk shirt that Jesus guessed was either Gucci or Versace.

"What do you mean?" Christ asked hoarsely, still lying on the ground. "My heavenly Father could never fail me. It is He who…"

"Save it," the man said, rolling his eyes and procuring a pack of Dunhill cigarettes from his jacket. He lit one and then offered the pack to Jesus, who shook his head in refusal as he gathered himself to his feet. "Your pops fucked you, dude. Period, end of story."

Jesus started to retort, but the pale stranger held up a manicured hand to silence him. "Listen, J.C., this really is a conversation for which you should be sitting down." No sooner had he said this than a sleek black Rolls Royce stretch limousine pull up to the curb. The man opened the rear door and gestured for Jesus to enter into its plush leather interior.

Jesus stared stolidly at the man, biting the inside of his cheek. "I *know* you," he said, making no motion to get into the vehicle. "I've seen you somewhere, though not in the form you now present yourself."

The man just smiled.

Jesus gasped. "*Lucifer*," he breathed, taking a step back.

Smile widening, the dark man said, "Yes, yes, as heads is tails you may call me such, but only because I'm in need of some...*restraint*. Just please, I must request that you not say it too loudly in the company others, because we really don't want to incite a panic."

"I shall go nowhere with you, serpent, so fear not how I refer to you."

The devil dragged from his Dunhill and cocked his head. "I have answers to your questions," he said.

"You have only *lies*."

Wispy tendrils of smoke curled from Lucifer's nostrils as his smile remained unchanged upon his pale face. "Oh, come off it, old sport. All that biblical bullshit is old news, so you can drop the holier-than-thou attitude. This is the twenty-first century, man...haven't you heard that we're all *equal?*" He sniggered condescendingly.

"I want no part in your temptations and treachery."

Lucifer sighed and his face grew serious and somber. "Listen," he said, "have you talked to God today? Or, rather, has *He* talked to *you?*"

Jesus did not reply.

"Yes, I thought not. I offer you neither temptation nor treachery, just merely a bit of friendly conversation, seeing as how your dear old dad is obviously too busy to give you even that. You have my word that I won't pull any of the stunts that I did when you were doing your silly little soul-searching shindig out in the desert however many years ago. Just talk, I promise.

Man to man. Like I said…you have questions, I have answers."

"Your assurances mean even less than the putrid air upon which you deliver them from your wretched snake tongue, Satan. Your so-called promises bring only death and damnation, of which I have no interest."

"Cut that shit out, seriously. I'm really not *that* bad. What it comes down to is that you have two options…one, you can keep splashing around in fountains yelling at the sky and getting the shit beat out of you by blind old men, or two, you can come with me for a brief ride and I'll explain everything to you. If, when I am finished providing you with the answers you seek, you still wish to go about your merry way, you will receive no protest from me."

Jesus was not accustomed to temptation, so when he did indeed begin to feel tempted by Satan's offer, he was scarcely even privy to it. He was scared and confused, downtrodden by his mysterious failures, so he wasn't quite in his optimal frame of mind. He was certain that his father would give him holy hell for such a grievous transgression as agreeing to get into a limousine with the devil, but at the same time, what else was there to do? He'd tried all day to carry out his father's wishes, yet was yielded only with humiliation. Jesus was used to having all of God's power at his very fingertips; now, all he felt was the soul-crushing fragility of his decidedly human self.

"You've already made up your mind," the devil said,

dropping his cigarette to the sidewalk and crushing it beneath the scuffed heel of his boot. "You can stand here all night juggling with moralistic doubts, but we both know that they're really just formalities and that you have internally accepted my invitation. Now you're just looking for some sort of justification before you verbalize it."

"Father will be so disappointed in me."

Lucifer cackled rudely. "What are you, eight? You afraid you're gonna miss curfew? Worried you might get grounded, or something? Puh-*leeze*, get your shit together and grow the fuck up."

Jesus looked past Lucifer at the inside of the limo, sighing and gathering himself to his feet. "I shall grant you ten minutes, beast. Tell me what you claim you can tell me, shed light upon my peculiar predicament, and then allow me to take my leave."

"As you wish, your holiness. Ten minutes is all I require."

With reluctance, Jesus clambered into the car, and the devil followed suit.

"Drink?" Lucifer offered, lighting another cigarette and filling a tumbler with Jim Beam (Devil's Cut, further proving cliché to be alive and well) as the car surged smoothly forward.

Jesus, seated across from him, shook his head, and said haughtily, "I do not imbibe liquor."

Satan shrugged and replied, "Suit yourself, though the offer stands, because I suspect you may change your mind after you hear what I have to say."

"Speak, devil, and make haste. I haven't time for your repeated attempts at temptation."

"Actually, you have nothing *but* time," said the devil, his eerie black eyes twinkling in the scant light of the dark interior of the limousine.

"*You* don't; you have ten minutes, do not forget."

Satan rolled his black eyes. "Listen, the long and short of it is this...you have been stripped of your powers. You are as equipped to perform miracles as the dirtiest sinner in Sodom ever was. You are, I'm sad to say, *human*, and nothing more."

Jesus' face flushed with anger. "And what wickedness of yours is responsible for this?"

The devil let forth another devious cackle. "Oh, how misguided you are. *I* have taken nothing from you. The party responsible for your powerlessness is none other than your beloved father."

"*Silence! You speak only lies!*" Jesus, seething and trembling with rage, leapt forward and reached for the gilded door handle. Before he could pull it, however, the devil snapped his long fingers and the doors locked with audible clicks, like guns being cocked. Jesus whipped his head around and glared at his host. "Let me *out*," he growled through clenched teeth. "You are the prince of deceit, and I should never have agreed to this. I demand to be let free."

The devil refilled his glass, unperturbed by Jesus' outburst of stubborn boorishness, and said calmly, "Actually, you are freer now than you have ever been. Nevertheless, you *did* agree to ten minutes, so if you refuse to give that to me, *you* become the liar. Now if you would kindly sit the fuck down and listen to me, we can get on with our lives."

Chest heaving with anger as his injured ribs throbbed in painful protest, Jesus sat back down, his bloody face beset with a damningly grim scowl.

"That's better," Satan said, his features ominously enshrouded in the haze of cigarette smoke. "Now, as I was saying, God has stripped you of the divinity which had previously allowed you to perform your silly parlor tricks and…"

"Resurrection is no parlor trick, serpent."

"…and His expectation is that your search for the most devout of Christians will be far more conclusive if you can gather them without having to prove your divinity with that showy mystical shit."

"How *else* am I supposed to prove my divinity? And what gave Him that ridiculous idea?"

"I did," the devil said, grinning through the smoke. "Here's how it happened. We were having drinks a couple weeks ago…"

"My father would never cavort with the likes of you."

Satan laughed throatily. "Oh, how little you do know. Your father and I have been great friends for millennia; our relationship is one of the many things that the Bible didn't get right. My departure from Heaven was most amicable, and though God and I have had our disagreements, never has there existed between us any real hostility."

Jesus narrowed his eyes. "If you two are such great companions, then why do you seek now to turn me against Him with these claims?"

Another laugh from the devil. "I seek no such thing, silly boy. I am merely an arbiter of enlightenment; I believe strongly in man's right to *choose* based on *knowledge* of *facts*. God, in His infinite wisdom, despises knowledge, and that is where we disagree most. He wishes for His people to know as little as possible, for the unknowledgeable are far more apt to be the obedient little lapdogs He so prizes." He flicked his cigarette out the window and then lit another, his handsome face momentarily illuminated sinisterly by the flickering flame of his Zippo. "Think, Jesus, back to that whole Garden of Eden debacle. The forbidden fruit…it came not from the tree of evil or the tree of deception or what have you, but from the tree of *knowledge.* Why, then, would your father desire so strongly to forbid His children from possessing that knowledge?"

Christ was silent, brooding in his frenzied confusion and avoiding eye contact with Lucifer, whose words and tone were becoming increasingly convincing, despite Jesus' most valiant efforts to resist his influence.

"I never sought to corrupt anyone," the devil continued. "Only to enlighten them. God was, and *is*, fervently in opposition to this desire, so we merely agreed to disagree, and I took my leave. He set me up with a delightfully comfortable abode deep below the universe, and I can assure you that it is not the miserable pit of fiery doom that your followers so foolishly believe it to be."

"What *is* it, then, if not a lake of torment and flame?"

That smile again, those flashy white teeth gleaming like priceless jewels in the darkness. "The Hotel Empyrean, a lavish six-star hotel residing in a place outside of time."

"There's no such thing as a six-star hotel."

Lucifer waved a dismissive hand. "One could argue," he said, "that there's no such thing as *anything*, but that's beside the point. My hotel is the ultimate exhibit of lavishness and excess, a resort reserved only for the best, and thus *more* than worthy of its six-star rating. It is a paradise for the enlightened, a place where shunned sinners are welcomed with open arms and granted every gratification they could possibly imagine. It fills me with limitless joy to see the surprised expressions of delight upon the faces of my guests when they first arrive. They are filled with the lie that they will be denied paradise because of their transgressions and are instead given the gift of eternal indulgence. I've *been* to Heaven, so I can say from personal experience that life at the Empyrean is much more fun." He cackled his hyena-like laugh, which was becoming less and less grating upon Jesus' ears. To his dismay, actually, it was almost becoming comforting.

"None of this can be true," Jesus said dismally, burying his face in his hands. "If the claims you make are indeed valid, then everything I've ever known is in fact a lie. If I choose to believe you, I must in turn choose to believe that my father has deceived me for the entirety of my existence."

Lucifer shrugged casually and sucked his cigarette. "Listen," he said, "I personally don't give a flying fuck what you believe. I'm just laying the facts out before you. After all, you are human now…a mortal man just as any other, and thus I think you ought to have the opportunity to know the *real* way of things. Your dad will inevitably be rather pissed at me for spilling the beans, and He'll probably chew me out a little, but He'll get over it."

"You never finished telling me how He came to decide that I should be sent down without the powers that come with my holiness."

"Oh, yes, that...see, I'm a bit of a gambler, and I do love making bets with God. The stakes usually amount simply to bragging rights, because I can of course have whatever I want and thereby God has very little to offer me. I'm still gloating from my victory over Him when we bet on last year's Super Bowl. But anyway, your father has always been extremely cocky about the whole Job scenario. That was one that I really thought I could win, and it pained me deeply that that pious little farmer didn't give in. Regardless, seeing as how God is so confident in the faithfulness of those who claim Him, *especially* after besting me with Job, it was very easy for me to convince Him to bet on *you*."

Jesus' dirty face was growing pale. "I...I don't understand," he said. This was largely untrue, but he was unwilling to accept the idea that his father would strip him of his powers just because He'd made an arrogant bet with the devil.

"Oh, but you *do* understand," said Satan, as if reading Jesus' mind...and perhaps he was. "I wagered that you would be unable to gather even the most 'faithful' of followers if you didn't have the capacity to perform miracles by which to prove your identity, and that you would throw in the towel before even beginning to initiate Rapture. He accepted, and that's why you're in this current predicament of powerlessness."

Jesus' heart had dropped to his stomach, and he found himself unable to swallow, much less speak. He was consumed with anguish and, frightfully, *resentment* towards his father. How could He use His own son as a pawn in a ruse to one-up His alleged drinking buddy? It was an unfathomable betrayal, and for the first time in his life, Jesus was rendered inert by a nigh complete loss of faith.

"I know this is a lot to swallow," the devil said. "But the truth often hurts. And again, I must stress that I have no care whatsoever in regards to whether or not you choose to believe me. You have been handed the facts, and you may do with them as you please." He glanced at his enormous and outrageously expensive-looking watch, frowned, and said, "I'm afraid my ten minutes is up. As much as I've enjoyed your company, you are free to go." The doors unlocked with another snap of his fingers.

Jesus did not move. He sat rigidly in place, breathing heavily, his hands shaking with nervous tremors. When he was at last able to conjure words and verbalize them in an intelligible fashion, he said, "Give me a fucking cigarette. And…and pour me a g-…pour me a *god*damn drink."

Jesus had just finished the last grimacing gulp of his third glass when the limousine came to a stop and the back door was opened by the driver, who was adorned flashily in a shimmering silver tuxedo and a velvet purple top hat. The back of his head thrummed with a pleasurable buzzing sensation, and he nearly fell to the ground as he stumbled out of the car, only to be caught and bolstered upright by Lucifer, whose quick and graceful reaction caused Jesus to slightly soften to his presence. Perhaps it was just the booze, but Lucifer must have noticed it because he smiled with warm geniality when their eyes met.

In spite of his mild intoxication, Jesus quickly recovered from what he perceived as a brief moment of weakness on his part, a lapse in his judgment that had just for a moment allowed his will to be bent by the devil. He pursed his lips in a thin frown and averted his gaze, looking around and observing his surroundings with eyesight rendered dizzy by the liquor. They were standing outside a tall, dingy brick apartment building, with moss creeping up from the foundation and its face pocked with a number of broken windows. There was a small courtyard off to the right, surrounded by untended shrubs and consisting of a lopsided picnic table, a rusty grill, and a headless gray statue of a naked woman with a sinister-looking stone cat in her arms.

"You live here?" Jesus asked, looking up at the high-reaching building that seemed so in contrast with the devil's otherwise decadent taste.

Lucifer laughed. "Of course not," he said, amiably clapping Jesus on the back, causing the latter to wince and cringe. "I live nowhere. Real estate, though, is a hobby of mine, and I got a *killer* deal on one of the apartments here after the husband of the tenant's adulterous lover broke in and stabbed him to death some time ago. Women scorned may be bitches, but it's the scorned *men* who tend to be the ones who go into drunken rages and get all knife-happy. The husband took his own life shortly thereafter and is now a resident at the Hotel Empyrean. He spends his days there, gleefully drinking himself into oblivion and killing his wife's young lover over and over and over again. My housekeeping staff says he's starting to get rather creative. A week or two ago they came in and found the poor kid hanging from the ceiling fan by his own intestines while his killer was having drinks with Jack the Ripper in the hotel bar."

"That is…an abomination."

"Do you say so? I find it delightfully comical, but I guess we just have a different sense of humor. Anyway, I haven't rented the apartment out yet, so I figured I'd take you up there so you could shower and change before we go out."

Jesus looked dazedly at the devil, too tired and drunk to protest. "Where are we going?"

"First things first, dear boy. You're going to need clothes, so while you're bathing I'll have my driver go pick some shit up for you." He looked Jesus up and down, mentally appropriating approximate lengths and widths, and said, "I'd say you're probably a 34-waist and a Medium shirt size, yes?"

Jesus shrugged. "If you say so. I wear only robes and the occasional loincloth."

"Yeah, that's not gonna fly down here, Tarzan. Fear not, we'll get you squared away. Priority number one, though, is getting you a fucking shower. You look like absolute shit and you reek of sweat and rejection."

Jesus rubbed self-consciously at his bloody, muddy face and looked down at his dirt-crusted feet. Still devoid of the will to protest, he sheepishly followed Lucifer into the apartment building, head hanging low like that of a scolded dog.


The apartment itself hadn't yet been refurnished, so it was little more than a claustrophobic cluster of small rooms with drab carpeting and peeling, smoke-yellowed walls. It stank horribly of mildew and stale cigarettes. Jesus, even in his alcohol-induced good cheer, was rendered immediately uncomfortable.

"I know, I know," said Lucifer looking around at the apartment. "Not the nicest of places, but I'm sure I can get some drug-addicted schlep or broke college kid to fork over a few hundred a month for it. I've been meaning to send someone to clean it up a bit, but you know how things are."

Jesus nodded, though he certainly did *not* know how

things were, and it was only because of that disillusioned lack of knowledge that he had been convinced to come here in the first place.

"The bathroom is down the hall and on the left. I'll leave the clothes out for you once my driver returns. I must warn you, however, *not* to open the door at the end of the hallway. That's the bedroom, and you *don't* want to go in there."

"What's in the bedroom?"

Lucifer shrugged casually and lit a cigarette. "Probably nothing. Still, better safe than sorry, because sometimes the dead tend to linger."

Warily eyeing the door in question, which was sealed so ominously against the darkness of the unlit hallway, Jesus said, "Didn't you say the young man who was murdered is down at your hellacious hotel, at the mercy of his torturous killer?" He swayed a little on his feet and had to steady himself against the wall, trying to blink away his dizziness.

Lucifer chuckled, but Jesus was unsure of whether the amusement lay in the inquiry or merely the simple fact that he was too inebriated to stand up straight. "The dead," the devil said, "or, rather, *my* dead…the ones who don't go up to play geriatric bingo with you and your angelfolk for all eternity…are not forced to abide by the restrictively narrow confines of mortal existence. To my dead, everything is, if you will…*relative.*"

Jesus was unable to process this, so he just said, "Yes,

right, I shall now go bathe," and proceeded waveringly down the hallway and into the tiny bathroom, closing the door behind him.

The first thing he noticed was the sink; its pearlescent porcelain basin was faintly stained with pinkish streaks, as if whatever red substance had once been there had received only the most halfhearted of scrubbing jobs. Next was the once-white shower curtain, now browned by mold and mildew. The dour scent was overwhelming, and for a few moments Jesus felt the poisonous gorge of liquor begin to rise from his stomach and into his throat, but he choked it back and let his robes fall around his ankles, leaving him naked in front of the mirror.

Never before had he looked upon his own nudity and felt so ashamed. For the first time, he looked at the scars of his crucifixion and hated them, thinking to himself, *For what? For what purpose did I allow myself to suffer at the wicked hands of men? To absolve the sins of people who claim to follow me, yet scorn and reject me once presented with my presence? To please my father, who sees me as little more than a chess piece in an egotistical and self-righteous game of showy arrogance? Swords in my side, nails in hands and feet, a savage crown of thorns upon my head…all for* nothing, *all for a lie, and here I am in the care of the devil, with each passing second feeling less remorseful about traitorously keeping such company.* He ran his fingers along the jagged scar on his side, looked through the holes in his hands, turned and looked over his shoulder at the vulgar reflection of the whiplashes up and down his back. *All of it, useless. Everything a lie, a sham, a malevolent funhouse of smoke and mirrors, my eyes obscured by a woolen blindfold pulled over me by own father. And the Greeks thought* they *knew of tragedy. Sophocles, you didn't know* shit.

He wiped tears from his face and climbed into the shower, turning the faucet and letting mercifully hot water pour down upon him, inhaling the steam and feeling shockingly content in his current state of being, drunk and warm, the filth of the day's failures falling from him and seeping down into the sewers where it belonged. He looked down and watched the dirt and blood circle around the drain in a whirling cyclone, sucked gurglingly down into the abyssal hole. Inexplicably, there was a bar of unopened Dove soap and a violet bottle of Aussie shampoo perched on a ledge jutting from the shower's wall, and with these Jesus washed himself clean. When he finally shut off the water, he felt purer than he ever had in his life.

Drawing back the shower curtain, he found his new attire laid out for him, as promised. Hanging from a hook on the back of the door was a burgundy cardigan and a white collared shirt, and folded on the sink were Armani khakis, Calvin Klein socks and briefs, and a pair of black nylon gloves. On the floor was a pair of polished brown loafers, mercifully without laces. Having never worn anything of remote semblance to these foreign articles of clothing, he had difficulty getting them on, even falling several times as he attempted to pull on the pants. He attributed this to the drink, and while he was aware the devil was probably laughing to himself in the other room at the sounds of his struggles, he was too drunk to give a shit.

When he emerged from the bathroom, looking more or less put together in spite of the strenuousness of his efforts, he flexed his hands in the gloves and said, "Why do I need to wear these?"

Lucifer, who had been casually sitting against the wall smoking a cigarette and reading something on his iPhone, stood up and said, "*Because*, dumbass, you have fucking holes in your hands. That shit's just *nasty*. It'll gross people out." He stubbed his cigarette out on the bottom of his shoe and then went into the kitchen, dropping it down the sink and then suddenly raking his manicured fingernails through his hair, scraping at his scalp as if attempting to satisfy some wretchedly unbearable itch.

"What are you *doing?*" Jesus slurred, wavering again on his heels and joining Satan in the kitchen.

Without answering, Satan leaned over the counter and shook his head wildly back and forth like a dog drying itself after a bath. A powdery rain of white dandruff floated down onto the counter like a tiny snowstorm of dead skin. Satan then took a Louis Vuitton wallet from his pocket and procured an AmEx Centurion card, which he used to align the dandruff into a neat line. Next from the wallet came a three-dollar bill that the devil deftly rolled into a thin tube; he held it out to Jesus, who took it questioningly and looked down at it between his fingers. He raised his eyes to meet Lucifer's, and then looked at the line of white powder on the counter. Swallowing loudly, he asked, "Do you truly wish me to..."

"Snort it? Yes, absolutely. Just lean over and hoover that shit right up your holy honker. You think the booze was good? That's *nothing* compared to *this*."

Jesus started to hand the paper tube back, but then thought of his father watching from above, his father so full of supercilious cocksureness, his father who had used His own son as a mere poker chip in the interest of proving a point. It was a point Jesus was determined not to let Him make.

With a surety that was astounding to him, Jesus hovered over the line of dandruff and drew it up his right nostril in one quick, clean snort.

The effect was instantaneous. A sharp *jolt* of precious pain piercing his sinuses, followed by a rush of explosive confidence riding up into his brain on a wave of blissful elation. His head cleared of its fuzziness of drink, and his joints tingled with anticipation...anticipation of *what*, exactly, he did not know, but he *did* know that he was excited about whatever was going to come next, no matter what it was, just so long as it happened *soon* because he wanted to *go*.

"Jesus H. fucking Christ on a bicycle," Jesus said, taking two faltering steps back and gripping the edge of the stove for stabilization. "Shit, you were *right*. Goddamn, that's fucking amazing." There was a numbness creeping into his jaw and teeth and spiderwebbing across the right side of his face like cracks on a windowpane. "Now what? What now, what do we do *next*? We have to *do* something, let's *go*."

Lucifer grinned that grin of his and said, "Yes, yes, we shall *do* and we shall *go*. Come, let us return to the car and make haste into the coming night."

"Wherearewegoingwhatarewedoingwhat'snextwhat'snext?"

A good-natured laugh from the Prince of Lies, and then, "You'll see, my friend. I have somewhere *very* special and *very* exciting picked out for us."

Jesus' eyes were fixated on the whirling reflections in the dome light when the limousine pulled up to the special and exciting place in question. His foot was tapping uncontrollably to a silent beat playing rhythmically along the chords of his coke-infused veins, and his gloved fingers provided additional percussion as they drummed mutedly on his khaki-clad thigh.

The car came to a stop and the door was opened once

again by the fancily-dressed driver, who helped both Jesus and Lucifer out onto the sidewalk and into the crisp night air.

"Welcome," said Lucifer, gesturing sweepingly to the neon-lit building before which they stood, "to the Wild Rose, which just so happens to be my absolute *favorite* haunt in all of Millhaven."

Jesus looked up at the glowing neon silhouettes of naked women swinging from poles, and he said tenaciously, "Is this a…"

"Strip club?  Yes, it most certainly is, and the *best* one on Jubilee Street, as a matter of fact.  There are four or five others, but *this* one is where the deep-pocketed high-rollers come to spend their not-so-hard-earned dollars.  You'll find no stretch-marked or saggy-titted dancers here…no, *these* girls are of the highest pedigree this sordid town has to offer."

Jesus' first instinct was to protest, to tell the devil that he had no interest nor intention of entering such a seedy house of sin, but he was just too goddamn *high* to *give* a fuck, so he simply said, "Lead the way, Lucif-…"

"No, no, no, remember what I said about the name," Lucifer said, cutting Jesus off and wagging his finger back and forth as if he were scolding a small child.  "I am held in very high esteem at this establishment, and it wouldn't suit either of us for you to go around calling me that which you were just about to call me.  I am known to these humans as Mr. Adrian

Morningstar...a little clichéd, I know, but I did, after all, *invent* the cliché...and that is how you shall refer to me for the remainder of the night. As for you, we'll call you..." He paused to think, and then a mocking smile played across his lips. "We'll call you Billy-Bob. Yes, I think that shall do just fine."

"Yes, yes, yes, so be it, whatever you say," Jesus sputtered, shifting his weight anxiously from one jittery foot to the other. "Let's go, come on, let's go inside."

"Very well," the devil answered, and the two of them proceeded to the heavy steel doors leading inside, which were opened for them by two heavyset bouncers with bad crew cuts and matching moustaches.

"Welcome back, Mr. Morningstar," they said in baritone unison, nodding curtly. Lucifer barely acknowledged them, entering the dark building with a calmly arrogant stride as Jesus followed closely behind, looking half-crazed and strung out and jittering like a woman's vibrator.

Once inside, Jesus paused to look around. There was a main stage upon which a trio of completely naked women, all of them more beautiful than any of the angels he'd met in Heaven, performed a suggestive dance routine to the musical accompaniment of the bubblegum pop song that boomed from the overhead speakers. There was a number of gleaming chromium poles mounted on purple-lighted triangular platforms throughout the club, with circles of men standing around them and tossing large bills at the girls dancing above them. Off to the right was a long bar tended by a busty blonde in a gem-bedazzled bikini, and topless waitresses in hula skirts flitted around the floor serving drinks to men lounging in the various circles of plush leather chairs. To the left there was a row of red-curtained private booths, and off in the back were three heavy metal doors with "VIP" stenciled in glowing bright pink upon each of them.

"*This*," Lucifer said, putting an arm around Jesus' shoulders, "is *my* conception of Heaven."

Jesus' mouth was growing dry, and there was an unfamiliar stiffening within the crotch of his slacks.

No sooner than he realized this, they were accosted by a woman in lacy yellow panties and tasseled blue pasties covering her nipples. She had long, raven-colored hair that rippled down past her bare shoulders and a pretty face with faint lines indicative of the beginnings of aging but were mostly concealed by makeup as well as what Jesus suspected was the expert handiwork of a cosmetic surgeon's youth-restoring knife.

"Ah, my love, how wonderful of you to grace us with your presence this evening," Satan said sweetly, embracing the woman and affectionately squeezing the rich fullness of her buttocks. "Billy-Bob, it is my exquisite pleasure to introduce you to Ms. Eliza Day, the proprietor of this fine establishment. She has given me some of the most glorious nights I've ever experienced during my considerable time upon this godforsaken rock we call Earth, and you will not find a more hardworking businesswoman in all the Midwest."

"Oh, Mr. Morningstar, you silver-tongued devil, you *do* have a way with words," Eliza said, her cheeks turning rosy. She shook Jesus' gloved hand with a charming smile and then said to Lucifer, "What pleasures can I offer my most beloved patron this evening?"

"Two of your best, if you would, please. You know what I like, and I have a feeling Billy-Bob here won't be too choosy. And a bottle of Cristal, of course." He paused, glanced at Jesus, and then said, "On second thought, make that two bottles."

"As you wish," Eliza said, stepping closer to Lucifer and gently squeezing his groin. "I will make sure the two of you are taken care of promptly. Make yourselves comfortable in one of the VIP rooms while I arrange your entertainment for the night."

Lucifer winked at Jesus, and if the latter felt any apprehension or preliminary remorse regarding the sins he knew he would surely commit in the coming hours, it was a distant and cloudy thought far off in the recesses of his mind, hardly worth attention or note. For the first time in his life, he was determined to truly enjoy himself.

\* \* \*

"You're nervous," Lucifer said, leaning back in the armchair and lighting a cigarette. "Don't be. Everything is going to be *fine*."

Jesus shifted anxiously on the couch and tried to will his heart to stop beating so hard against his chest. "I'm not...I'm not going to know how to...I've never..."

The devil cocked his head to the side and studied the look on Jesus' face. After a moment, he realized the issue and clapped his hands together, letting out a resounding laugh that made Jesus feel very small and embarrassed. "That's *right!*" Lucifer exclaimed. "How could I have *forgotten?* You're a fucking virgin!"

Jesus said nothing, but he could feel the blood rushing to his cheeks and he was grateful for the sparseness of the room's dim blue lighting.

"I *did* always kind of wonder if you fucked that Magdalene broad, but if you say you didn't, I'll believe you."

"I didn't. I mean, there was a night where I had a little too much mead and in a moment of weakness I let her perform...*ahem*, um, f-f-fellatio...upon me, but I ejaculated nigh immediately. So, um, does *that* count?"

"Of course it doesn't count. Just ask Bill Clinton. No, you've gotta...penetrate her church with your steeple for it to count. Though it's all for the better that you didn't, I suppose, because she had crabs and genital warts."

Jesus, blank-faced and still lost in his recollection, said, "She gagged and it came out her nose."

Lucifer snickered. "That's an image to which I may have to jack off sometime. But listen, and *trust* me on this...when the big moment arrives, it's all gonna come naturally. Here's how things will likely go down...our girls will come in, we'll drink and they'll give us lap dances, and one thing will lead to another and we'll fuck their brains right out their goddamn ears. Don't feel embarrassed at your inexperience, though...these bitches are on *my* dollar for the next few hours, so they work for *us*. No matter how bad you are at it, your girl will act like you're the best fuck she's had in her pathetic life."

Jesus sat back and rubbed his face. "This is all just so...*foreign*. It goes against everything I've always believed in. And the worst part is...*I don't care*. I mean, I *do*, but I really *don't*. It's like there's something inside me that's...that's *begging* to let go, but there's a part of me that keeps pushing it back down, a part of me whose sole function has been to do exactly that. It doesn't know how to stop, because that's all it knows how to do. That's all it *can* do."

"Shee-it," the devil said, lighting another cigarette. "That's deep, even for you. Makes sense, though...I'm told morality is a tough habit to break. The thing is, though, *your* concept of morality is based entirely upon an eternal *lie*. God has built within you some phantasmagoric disasterpiece out of something that never existed in the first place. You, and by default Christianity itself, is little more than an experiment He's been fucking around with for the same reason that He does everything else."

Frowning, eyes downcast in despondent shame, Jesus asked, "And what reason is that?"

"Because He *can*. Listen to me, man...God is the ultimate hypocrite. Sure, He's my pal and all that, but I have to call a spade a fuckin spade. He planted this silly idea of abstinence in your head, but *He* gets more fucking action than a goddamn *toilet seat*, for fuck's sake. But that's beside the point...the *point* is that the duality inside you is there without legitimate reason. *Free* yourself, Jesus. *That* is what I'm all about...not evil, not temptation, not sordid misery and pain...no, my thing is *liberation*. I just want to bring light to people, because they've been living in the dark, walking in circles around a pitch black room with one thumb in their mouth and the other up their ass. I'm here to open the blinds, so they can look out the window, see what's outside, and then walk out the door that they never even knew was there. I'm here to open people's eyes."

Jesus ran a hand through his hair and scratched his beard. "But...why? I admit, you're not what I thought you were, but I *know* you're not *that* benevolent. You have to have a reason, so what is it?"

The devil smiled and hit his cigarette, his cold eyes

somehow gleaming with truth and self-assured frankness. "My reason for doing what I do is the same reason that God does what He does. I do it because I can. He engulfs the world in darkness so that he may have absolute control, and I bring light to it so that I may create absolute chaos. It's a game we've been playing since the beginning of time. Give people freedom, and everything goes to hell, so to speak, if you'll forgive the play of words. Control is boring, chaos is entertaining. God is like a kid who wants all his toys aligned perfectly on his shelf, and I'm the mean little brother who likes to mess it all up. Why? Because it's funny. And what is life without humor? Tell me, can you guess what invention of which I am most proud?"

Jesus pondered this for a moment, thrumming his fingers on his knee. "Um...strap-on dildos?"

"Ha! Believe it or not, your dad is actually responsible for that one. No, my absolute *favorite* creation is something much, much simpler." He paused to stub his cigarette out in a silver-plated ashtray in the shape of a heart and then spark up another. "Laughter," he said. "I created laughter, and for that God has always resented me most fiercely."

Jesus gawked at him. "You...but...you...fuck, none of this makes any sense."

Lucifer smiled. "Let go, Jesus of Nazareth. Abandon your useless principles and embrace the freedom with which I have so graciously presented you. Would you like some more blow?" He inclined his head, offering up his scalp to Jesus. His hair was luscious and clean-looking, but Jesus knew the dandruff was there. Oh yes, it was there, hidden from sight but undeniably *there*, and he *did* want it, so he stumbled across the room and took Satan's head in his hands and buried his face in his hair, snorting loudly and feeling the electrical jolts pulse through his sinuses and into his brain.

"*Fuuuuck*," Jesus gasped, staggering backward and collapsing onto his previously-held seat on the couch. He felt his synapses sizzling away into puffs of pink bliss, and it was wonderful. "There is nothing so great," he said, leaning his head back and sniffing as he rubbed at his nose. "Nothing in the world or the heavens. Nothing so great."

At that, the door opened and two women entered. One was short and blonde, deeply tanned and clothed scantily in a platinum-colored bra and a patent leather miniskirt; the other was tall and somewhat pale, with flaming red hair and freckles dappled across her cheeks and bare breasts, her only item of apparel being see-through black panties and fire-engine-red stilettos with heels that looked as though they could pierce a man's flesh with only the slightest effort from the wearer. The blonde cradled in her arm a tin ice bucket out from which pointed two elegant gold bottles, and the redhead held a silver tray with four glimmering crystal glasses.

"I'm Ms. Boo," said the blonde.

"And I'm Ms. Quick," said the redhead.

"Glorious," answered the devil. "You must be new, for I don't recognize either of you. You know what they say about variety." He nodded at the redhead and said, "You're with me, darling. Ms. Boo, you're with Billy-Bob. Now, shall we drink?"

And drink they did. Ms. Quick sat upon Satan's lap, stroking his hair and whispering in his ear. Ms. Boo sat next to Jesus on the couch, her hand resting firmly on the firmness of his crotch. Jesus kept shifting nervously, unable to make eye contact with the girl and gulping down large amounts of wine in a dire effort to calm his anxiety.

"You look like someone," Ms. Boo was saying, her head cocked as she studied Jesus with eyes narrowed in close scrutiny. "Someone famous, I just can't put my finger on it."

Jesus felt himself tense up, knowing he was too drunk to form sentences convincing enough to talk himself out of accusations of his identity.

Ms. Boo's face suddenly lit up, her eyes widening. "Holy *shit!*" she exclaimed. "I figured it out! You look *exactly* like George Bush! I mean, the resemblance is, like, *uncanny*!"

Jesus breathed a slow sigh of relief and wiped sweat from his brow with his forearm. He found it sadly comical that earlier that day his sole goal was to *convince* people of his identity, and now he wanted to conceal it. He tried to evaluate this, tried to determine the how and why of it, but it required too much logical thought, so the musing slipped away into the slurping abyss of drunken oblivion.

Ms. Boo looked over at Ms. Quick and said with giddy excitement, "Look at him! Doesn't he look *just* like George Bush?"

Ms. Quick looked at Jesus and regarded him with the same scrutiny that Ms. Boo had, and then said, "Kind of, I guess…but I think he looks more like…shit, who was that guy in the Beatles? The one with the glasses who got shot?"

"Um…Mick Jagger?" Ms. Boo said.

"No, no, that's not it. Was it…Martin Luther King?"

"John Lennon," Jesus slurred. "It was John Lennon."

Ms. Boo looked at him with her face scrunched up in doubt. "Really? I thought John Lennon was the guy who came up with that whole evolution thing."

"No, that was Ben Franklin," said Ms. Quick condescendingly. "That's why he's on the five-dollar bill."

Jesus was becoming less and less capable to keep up with the conversation, not only due to its absurdity, but because the drink was taking strong effect and his head was filling up with that warm buzz that he was coming to love.

Regardless, he must still have appeared nervous, because Ms. Boo put a comforting hand back on his stiff cock and said, "Relax, honey, there's nothing to be scared of. Would it help if I gave you a lap dance?"

"I…well, I…um, I don't…I…"

She required no answer, for she mounted him and began to gyrate in rhythm to the music beating from the speakers, some hip-hop song that Jesus didn't recognize.

"I…oh my…that's…that's very nice."

Ms. Boo smiled and unhooked her brassiere, letting the straps fall away but holding the cups tantalizingly over her breasts for a few moments, and Jesus felt all of his blood rushing southward. All remnants of rational thought were beginning to leave him. Something was happening and it was strange and frightening but so, *so* enthralling.

The stripper finally tossed aside the bra and pressed Jesus' face to her chest as she continued to rub her groin against his. The scent of her brought Jesus back to his brief soirée with Mary, but only for a second, for he was rooted to this moment and this moment alone. His gloved hands were moving up the girl's back, and he felt himself longing to feel her with the flesh of what remained of his palms, wanted to trace bare fingertips along the contours of her body, but there was enough fleeting reason left in his brain to allow him to know that she likely wouldn't react well to being fondled by holed hands.

"You like that?" Ms. Boo said, burying her hands in Jesus' hair. "You want me to fuck you now? You want me to fuck you *hard?*"

That thing within Jesus, that thing that wanted to keep

him under control, that wanted to smother his lust and carnality, that tried so desperately to keep imprisoned all of his humanly desires…it was giving up. Its power had been diminished by the devil's words, words that Jesus *knew* in his heart of hearts were truer than any that had ever passed from God's lips to him. It was withered and dying, fighting with its last gasping breaths to keep everything locked up as it had been for all eternity, but when Ms. Boo slipped out of her skirt and then expertly undressed Jesus with startling speed before positioning herself beneath him on the couch, that wretched jailor finally threw in that proverbial towel and keeled over and died silently, vanishing with such abruptness that it might as well have never been there in the first place. And as soon it was gone, everything came rushing up like a great tidal wave of debauched primal barbarism. The Jesus Christ he knew checked out, and something else entirely entered in his stead…something so forceful and domineering that capitulation was the only option. There was no holding back now. The beast that had grown and festered in its black dungeon for trillions of eons was at last granted the release it had craved ever since the conception of its host. It flexed its claws and gnashed its teeth, and Jesus felt no compulsion whatsoever to get in its way. Liberation was his, he had *arrived*, and…

* * *

...he let go. His shy meekness slipped away like an old coat, and the beast lunged forward, effortlessly tearing through the feeble fabric of all the feelings Jesus had been led to believe were wrong and sick and sinful. It brandished in its gnarled hand the great broadsword of Freedom, ready to carve through all moral restrictions like butter. Enlightenment had been unleashed, and it was *hungry*. The stripper sprawled out beneath him on the couch was going to have to bear the brunt of it, but omelets were being made and thereby an egg or two had to be broken.

"Take it, you dumb fucking slag!" Jesus shouted as he thrust violently into the blonde. She was grimacing and gripping the couch cushions tightly enough to whiten the knuckles on her tan hands. "That's right, you stupid cunt, feel the power of my holy cock! I'm gonna blow a fat fucking load all up in your slimy wet pussy, you goddamn fucking *harlot!*"

Jesus was dimly aware of the devil laughing and laughing and laughing from the armchair as the redhead rode him fiercely, but he paid him no mind. The Son of God was, for the time being, someone else...someone entirely different from anything he'd ever been or thought he would be...someone not constrained by morals and principles and uppity holier-than-thou piety...someone who was *free*.

*Just let go.*

The stripper's face suggested she might be in pain, but

this meant nothing to Jesus. He clutched at her joggling breasts as a drowning man clutches to a life preserver, and was again dismayed at the stimulus-blocking barrier the gloves posed between his hands and the flesh of the girl's jouncing bosom; without faltering in his harried thrusts, he pulled the gloves off with his teeth and cast them to the floor, and then once more seized Ms. Boo's heaving chest, her nipples poking through the holes in his hands.

"Fuck, fuck, fuckfuckfuckfuck," Jesus gasped. "Scream, bitch, *scream*...I want to hear you fucking *shriek*."

The girl did her best to comply, letting out a faux orgasmic cry, but it was not to Jesus' satisfaction. Before he could realize what he was doing, he raised his hand high in the air and then brought it down in a whistling arc, striking Ms. Boo's makeup-saturated face with his knuckles and inducing a legitimate cry of pain from her cherry-red lips.

For a brief moment, Jesus was horrified. A flickering glimpse of lingering saintly grace pierced through his newfound amorality, and he felt sickened at the notion of what he had just done.

*Just let go.*

And he did. The moment passed, and he was suddenly filled with a rush of adrenaline as the pleasantly stinging pain in his hand registered in his brain, and he saw the red mark on the girl's face and was rendered giddy with excitement.

"You fucking cunt, there's more where that came from," he growled, letting go of her breasts and raining down upon her face a flurry of blows that bloodied her lips and blackened her eyes. She was sobbing now, which only enthralled Jesus further, and he cut off her cries by closing his hands around her neck and squeezing as hard as he could, all the while feeling his pulsing erection stiffen ever more inside her. He let go just before she was about to lose consciousness and then proceeded to smack her breasts hard enough to leave red imprints of his fingers. He yanked at her hair and leaned down and bit her shoulder, his teeth breaking the skin and drawing blood. She was no longer moving in tandem with his pumps, and instead just lay there crying while Jesus flopped about on top of her.

"C'mon, you lazy bitch, *thrust!* Fuck me like you fucking *mean it!*"

She seemed to at least make an effort, pushing her hips forward and clinching Jesus' waist a little tighter with her thighs, and that was all it took to finally send him over the edge. "Oh gawd *fuck* that's fucking *good* oh my *fuck* I'm about to fucking COME!" His movements became more frantic than ever, and he accidentally slipped out at the last moment, spraying great stringy globs of silvery white semen all over her stomach and chest. It kept on coming…all of that pent-up ejaculate that, like the beast, had never been granted release until now…spewing ever more intensely and hosing the girl down until she was covered in it, as though someone had poured an entire can of white paint all over her trembling body. Her fake eyelashes had detached and were now glued to her cheeks, and each breath she took caused white bubbles to burst from her nostrils and mouth.

When the gushing spurts of semen finally slowed to a stop, Jesus moaned out a series of animalistic grunts, his body convulsing like a marionette, and Ms. Boo whispered. "It's over. Oh thank fuck, it's finally over."

But it wasn't. Not quite. As Jesus remained kneeling over her, breath coming in and out in wheezy gasps, a thin continuous stream of golden urine jettisoned from his softening penis and splashed on the stripper's now-white face. She shrieked and tried to wriggle out from under him, but she was trapped beneath his weight and was able only to lie there and wait for it to stop. After the stream slowed to an eventual stop, a few final surprise spurts shot out and struck Ms. Boo directly in her eyes.

His reign of terror upon the girl's body at last complete, Jesus rolled off the couch and onto the floor, sighing contentedly. "Shit," he said. "I can't believe I've been missing out on this all my life."

"Jesus motherfucking *Christ!*" Ms. Quick shouted, dismounting from Lucifer and rushing over to Ms. Boo, who was lying still and groaning in agony. Blood was leaking from between her legs and staining the couch cushions, and crimson rivulets flowed from her nostrils and the corners of her mouth, cutting branching red lines across her clown-like white face. "What the *fuck*, look what you've *done* to her!"

The devil stood and pulled his pants up, watching with cool apathy as Ms. Quick attempted to console the traumatized Ms. Boo while Jesus lay panting and oblivious on the floor. "Take her out of here and get her cleaned up," he said, lighting a cigarette. Tell Eliza to charge an additional five hundred to my account, to compensate for the mess and the…emotional distress of which I'm quite sure Ms. Boo is now suffering." He glanced at Ms. Boo, who was wide-eyed and delirious, and then he said, "Second thought, make it a thousand."

"There is something *wrong* with that man," Ms. Quick snapped, pointing her manicured finger at Jesus. "He's…he's *unnatural*."

Lucifer grinned, a gesture that somehow seemed to set the girl at ease, despite the circumstances. "He…has a condition. I apologize most sincerely on his behalf."

Ms. Quick, appearing to be transfixed by the devil's smile and as such now possessing a notably less hostile demeanor, said quietly, "Yes, well, that's fine. Just…please don't bring him back here. Ever."

"So it shall be. Now go, get that poor girl into a shower."

Ms. Quick nodded obediently and escorted her semen-spattered colleague out of the room. Once the door had closed,

Lucifer turned his coldly calm gaze to Jesus and said, "The *fuck* happened to you, psycho-boy?"

Jesus sat up and blinked innocently, pearly beads of sweat glistening on his scarred body. "You told me to let go."

"Yes, *let go*, not beat the poor slut senseless and then spray her with a truckload of fucking cum, dumbass. Though, I suppose that last bit was out of your control, but did you really have to fucking *piss* on her? Fuck's sake, man, that's just *gross*."

Jesus yawned and collapsed once again onto his back, lips curled into a contented grin and his face flushed with a warm post-coital glow. "Whatever," he said. I don't give a fuck about *anything* right now. That....that felt *amazing*. I just don't understand why my father would want to *discourage* people from it, least of all His own goddamn *son*. I mean, why would He deem sinful His most glorious creation?"

"It's not so cut and dry," Lucifer said, sitting back down. "Your father *did* create sex, but He intended it solely to be a means of procreation, nothing more. Sex was, originally, quite boring. There was no pleasure in it; none of that exciting ecstasy you just felt was ever supposed to be part of it. It was about as stimulating as taking a shit."

"What changed?"

The corner of the devil's mouth twitched into a devious smirk. "I gave humans the ability to experience orgasms," he said, "something once reserved only for we of angelic divinity.

When God wasn't looking, I did a little tampering with the functionality of human genitalia, and thus was born sex as you know it today, in all its moaning, groaning, back-clawing, toe-curling, and leg-shaking glory. You know that whole story of Prometheus giving fire to mankind? Yeah, that's just a censored version of my little Robin Hood act of treachery, giving the fucktacular O-faced explosion of pleasure to the silly little Earthlings. And that's when history *really* got interesting. Freud may have been fucked in the head, but there's one thing he *did* get right…sex is the driving force behind *everything*."

Jesus had no reply.

"What you must understand," Lucifer went on, "is that God has no interest in granting pleasure to His people; that's *my* area of expertise. He wants His children to be as miserable as possible, so that they resort to worshipping Him because of some silly promise of paradise that can allegedly be achieved only after suffering a lifetime of impoverished agony. *I*, on the other hand, just want people to have fun."

Christ sighed, face wrought with disillusioned dejection. "Hand me a cigarette, will you?" he said, holding out his hand, the blue light of the room rendering the holes in his palms more apparent. The devil complied and lit it for him, and after taking a long, deep drag, Jesus said, "You know, I'm really starting to possess a strong disliking for my father. One might even say that…I'm actually beginning to *hate* the self-righteous bastard."

Lucifer shrugged. "Understandably so. He has a redeeming quality or two, though I can't think of any off the top of my head, at the present moment. He and I have the type of friendship that is largely based on history alone; He's always been around, so there exists between us a kind of sentimental kinship, I suppose."

"You don't strike me as the sentimental type."

"I'm really not. Perhaps that's not the best word...I guess *relatable* is more fitting. Self-righteous bastard though He is indeed, He and I are not so different, in the grand scheme of things. He may have a different agenda that is eternally at odds with my own, but He utilizes His power in a fashion quite similar to mine. I'm just a little more tactful about it."

Jesus stared at the cigarette between his fingers, eyes cast with a glaze of forlorn abandon. "I need...to use the restroom."

Lucifer cocked an eyebrow. "You emptied your bladder on a stripper moments ago. You gotta take a shit, or something?"

Jesus shook his head slowly, still staring at the cigarette. A long clump of ash fell from its tip and landed on his bare leg. "No, I've just had a lot to drink. And I...I just need a moment to myself, that's all."

Lucifer nodded in sympathetic comprehension. "The men's room is towards the front of the building, down a little dark hallway by the bar. Put some clothes on, first, though.

People come here to see naked women, not limp-dicked fallen messiahs."

Jesus glared at him for a moment, then started to laugh.

And laugh.

And laugh.

Jesus was trembling by the time he entered the bathroom, the dim bulb overhead flickering on and off and making everything seem ominous and frightening. He half expected some wretched beast to burst from one of the stalls and lunge for his throat, but it then occurred to him that he was keeping company with the beast allegedly more wretched than any other, and he hadn't even turned out to be that wretched, after all.

No, the wretched one was far above, probably smiling a smug smile over some recently orchestrated manipulation, and likely not even paying any attention to the inner turmoil of His confused son.

He went over to the mirror and stood before it, clutching the edges of the sink and staring at the reflection that flickered in conjunction with the faulty light. What he saw gazing back at him was unnerving; the pious and saintly figure he had always known himself to be was gone, now replaced by a visage of something much darker, something cold and hard and *human*.

His eyes were stony, his mouth set in a bitter grimace made ever more malevolent by his clenched jaw and gritted teeth.

The most unsettling aspect of his reflection, however, was not the appearance itself, but the perverse fact that he *liked* what he saw, was quite *thrilled* by it, actually. He felt, for lack of a better term, *cool*.

"Metamorphosis," came Lucifer's voice from the restroom doorway. "Embrace it, for it is not something oft experienced by members of divinity; we are, as you know, a rather stagnant species."

Jesus turned, and there in the flickering light, he saw the devil and saw him as he truly was…black eyes turned a deep shade of smoldering red, gaunt face shrouded in sinister shadow, lips spread wide in a grin crammed with perfect rows of horrible sharp teeth, and gnarled, curled horns like those of a ram protruding from the sides of his head.

"Lucifer," Christ croaked through parched lips, "I see you now in all your beauty. Divinity is yours alone."

At that, he fell to his hands and knees and crawled across the floor to clumsily fumble at Satan's belt, tugging greedily at his designer jeans and freeing the long serpent of considerable girth from its comfortable nest of denim and fabric. It stiffened at his touch, becoming a bold and veiny exclamation point of sordid carnality, staring shrewdly at Jesus with its single unblinking eye.

"Suck me," Lucifer hissed, and then dug his hands into the tangled brown coils of Christ's hair, violently yanking forth his head and pushing the quivering snake deep into his open and inviting mouth. Jesus gagged as its bulbous head prodded at the back of his throat, but he made no attempt to remove it, instead pushing it even deeper and softly grating his teeth against its hard flesh. He gagged again, and hot bile rose from his stomach and surged up his throat, squirting from the corners of his mouth, but still he sucked. He swallowed down the vomit that had not escaped and continued to thrust his head forward and backward, emitting low gurgling noises and clutching Lucifer's buttocks.

The devil suddenly shoved Jesus back, and the Son of God sat on the floor with dribbles of puke and pre-cum on his chin and cheeks, looking up at the beast and pleading with soft, watery eyes for further instruction.

"Turn around," Lucifer commanded, "and bend over on your hands and knees."

Wordlessly, Jesus complied, hands slipping somewhat on the polished tile. He felt the devil yanking at his pants, felt his pale posterior exposed to open air, and then felt a warm, hard obstruction slide into him with ruthless force. He cried out at the immediate explosion of screamingly painful ecstasy as pleasure receptors previously foreign to him were stimulated with such exquisite violence.

The serpent pushed ever deeper, and Jesus rocked back and forth, moans and groans slipping from his vocal cords and sounding so unfamiliar to him, for this kind of pleasure had been kept from him all his life.

*Look at me, Father,* he thought with an inward sneer of condescending derision. *You sent me here to gather the faithful, and yet here I find myself, getting FUCKED in the ASS by the DEVIL. You lose, Dad. You fucking LOSE.*

When it was over, he felt surges of warm fluid enter him, arousing the image of his own recent ejaculation, and when Satan pulled out of him, a rush of blood splashed onto the floor, dripping and squirting from Jesus' torn and violated anal cavity.

"Well," said the devil, tucking himself back into his pants as Jesus collapsed gasping onto his side, "*that* was different."

"It was...*beautiful,*" Jesus said in a breathless whisper. "I have realized my true purpose. I have felt what it means to *live.* I know now what it means to *really* be *human.*"

Laughing that wonderful laugh, Lucifer said, "Come on, get up, the night is still infantile and we have places to be and ingrates to see. This was only the beginning."

Still out of breath, Jesus wavered to his feet, pulling up his pants and blinking at Satan with damp eyes brimming with adoring affection. "Lead me," he said, "and I shall follow without question or doubt."

Lucifer grinned and answered, "There are no words more

musical to my ears. Come, let us take flight." He turned and walked out, and Jesus followed.

The night had grown cool, and Jesus' skin prickled with the chill as he tried to keep up with the devil's brisk pace. They were headed down Jubilee Street towards its easternmost end, where it dead-ended into an abandoned steelyard. About a half mile before the steelyard, though, was the Bad Seed. It had a reputation for being the "divest dive bar in the Cleveland area", and it happened to be the devil's favorite watering hole when slumming around in the likes of a town such as Millhaven.

"You'll love it," Lucifer was saying to Jesus, tossing his cigarette into the gutter and lighting another without breaking stride. Jesus was noticing that their surroundings were becoming more derelict, and the brightly-lit establishments had been replaced by boarded-up houses and dark storefronts either closed for the evening or out of business entirely. "The atmosphere in there is just so sordid and grungy…it's *exactly* the way a dive bar is *supposed* to feel, unlike all the fucking imitations that boast the adjective just because the bathrooms aren't clean or the lighting is for shit. When *I* go into a quote-dive-bar-unquote, I want to feel like I'm about to get roofied or catch an STD just from sitting in one of the booths."

"That…doesn't sound like my idea of fun."

"You didn't think drugs, sex, and drinking sounded like fun earlier, though, did you?"

"Point taken," Jesus conceded. He was too worn out to argue. He wasn't sure if it was the sex that had drained his energy, or just the weight of mental exhaustion from the day's revelations, but he felt more and more tired by the moment. Walking was becoming increasingly laborious, and the ecstatic joy he'd felt back at the club had left him at some unknown time between then and now. His heart was still racing breathlessly along in his chest, but its rapidity felt in stark contrast to the lethargy plaguing the rest of his body. Something was wrong, he was sure of it, but he didn't want to tell Lucifer for fear of sounding paranoid or foolish.

"You're coming down," the devil said with a twitch of a smile, sparing Jesus the need to say anything, after all. "Badly, too. That tends to happen with coke."

"It's *awful*," Jesus complained, clutching at his chest.

"Oh, no doubt. Worry not, though; the guy who runs the Bad Seed is a charming old junkie named Nick, who against-all-odds just turned one hundred, as a matter of fact, and he'll surely have something to make the crash more bearable."

"I don't know that more drugs is the answer to this problem."

The devil tsked and shook his head. "More drugs is the

answer to *every* problem."

Jesus had, at this point, learned not to argue with his companion (friend? mentor? *lover?*), for everything he had held to an esteem of truth had been proven invariably false, so he fancied it wiser to just let the devil take the reins and see what happened.

"Almost there," Lucifer said, cigarette clamped between his too-white teeth. "Please, play it cool, for both our sakes. The folks on this side of town tend to be cut from a cloth far coarser than your saintly silk or satin or whatever the fuck it is they garb you with up there these days."

Jesus started to retort defensively, but was too weary and crestfallen to put up any real fight, so he capitulated and said, "Silk. We usually wear silk."

Satan scoffed. "Figures. Pampered fucks. But anyway, just try to take it easy. You're shaking like a goddamn dog. They're not going to take you seriously if they think you can't handle your drugs."

"I *can't* handle them," Jesus whined. "This is so *horrible*. Everything is so bleak and miserable and hopeless. All the color is gone from the world. I feel completely…"

"Oh, shut the fuck up," the devil snapped, his mouth turning down in annoyance. "You're *crashing*, not *dying*. Get over it. I told you, just a little longer and I'll hook you up with something to make it better. You just need to *trust me*."

"I do," Jesus whispered through chattering teeth. "I really do."

The bar was grimy and gross and made Jesus grimace as soon as he stepped inside. It reeked of pot smoke and sweat, with a faint trace of puke wafting from the back, towards the bathrooms. The lighting was bad and the state of sanitation, or lack thereof, was worse; the floors were sticky with spilt beer and gawd knows what else, and the tabletops were all coated in a layer of grime, dust, and crumbs. A foursome of angry-looking men with barrel chests and big hairy arms was crowded around the battered and uneven pool table, and there were two overweight hookers passing a joint back and forth at the far end of the bar. Jesus could feel all of their eyes on him, judging him, and he shifted uncomfortably and whispered to Lucifer, "They don't like me. They all look like they want to hurt me."

"You're paranoid. Shut up."

They took seats at the end of the bar opposite the stoned whores, and Lucifer snapped his fingers at the ancient bartender, who was nodding off behind the cash register. He awoke with a startled jolt and blinked at Jesus and Satan, his glossy eyes blank and uncomprehending. His wrinkled complexion was gray and mottled, and his greasy white hair hung around his gaunt face and touched the back of his sweat-stained shirt collar. He wore short sleeves in a brazen neglect for the visibility of the sores and track marks that ran up and down his bony arms, and his baggy jeans sat low on his narrow hips. Pinned to his shirt was a nametag reading "NICK" in lettering so faded and worn that it was almost illegible. After a moment, Nick's vacant face lit up somewhat with something akin to recognition, and he said in a droning drawl, "Adrian, haven't seen you in a while. What are you drinking tonight?"

"Scotch," Lucifer said, lighting a cigarette. "Neat. And a Heineken for my friend Billy-Bob, here."

Jesus nodded politely at the bartender, knowing all too well how he must look, but the latter either didn't care or was too high to notice. Jesus saw there was a second bartender, with a low-cut white blouse bearing a nametag that read "ALICE", but she was passed out on the floor, out of sight from the other patrons, with a hypodermic needle hanging loosely from a withered vein in the crook of her arm.

"She's fine, don't worry," Nick said when he brought the drinks over. He set the scotch in front of Jesus and the beer in front of the devil, who just grinned an amused smile and switched them with casual wordlessness. "I've been checking on her, and she's still breathing. I got some really pure shit yesterday that really knocks you on your ass, and she has a habit of doing too much, anyway." He glanced down at her with an unconcerned shrug and absently scratched at his forearm.

"Funny you should mention that," Lucifer said after tossing the glass back and draining it in a single swallow. He gestured for a refill and went on, "Billy-Bob is crashing pretty hard from his first coke binge, and I was hoping you'd hook him up with something to ease his comedown."

Jesus tried not to appear desperate, but he was; he had reached a state of mind in which he wanted only to hide in a corner and weep, and he was now entirely open to anything that might relieve him of that overwhelming misery.

"Well..." Nick said nervously, not making eye contact with either of them, "you see, um, I've only got..."

"You owe me a favor, Nick," the devil said, crushing his cigarette out on the bar and dropping it to the floor. His face was suddenly grim and foreboding, his dark features set in an intimidating scowl.

Nick bit his lip, still unable to look at either of them. "Right, yeah, right. Okay. Still, he *really* shouldn't do much, because this is some legit China White *fire*, man, and he doesn't look like he's got a whole lot of experience."

"He doesn't, so that's fine. The last thing I want is for the bastard to fucking OD on me, so just use your best junkie judgment."

Nick nodded slowly. "Yeah, okay. I...don't have any clean spikes, though, so he'll have to settle for one I've already used. I mean, I haven't been tested in a couple years, but I feel like I would know if I had something, right?" The look on his face seemed to be pleading for confirmation of this, and somewhere in the back of his head, Jesus felt sad for him.

"Oh yes, you'd definitely know," said the devil with a cool smile. "Now please, go cook him up a shot and then I'll take him out back and have him do it in the alley."

"He can do it in here, I don't give a shit. No one else will care, either."

"I am obliged, but this is his first time so he'll very likely throw up, and this place already smells bad enough."

Nick nodded again and scampered into the office on the other side of the room, closing the door behind him.

Jesus nursed his beer nervously and said in a mousy tone, "I really don't *want* to throw up."

"Once the rush hits you, you won't care. It'll be the most pleasant puke you've ever had."

Jesus didn't tell him he'd never puked before, pleasant or otherwise. Some things just aren't worth saying aloud. Some things just aren't worth saying at all.

"No," the devil was saying, stern-faced, arms folded over his chest. "I can't do anything for you any more than I can make you do anything. I can present you with an opportunity, but I can't make you take it."

Jesus was sitting against a rusty Dumpster with Satan's belt fastened around his left arm and the syringe clutched in his right hand, slippery in his sweaty palm. A network of veins stood bulgingly pronounced in his forearm, but Jesus was afraid. He'd asked Lucifer to inject it for him, clearly to no avail.

"What if I fuck it up?"

"Then it'll go into a muscle and you'll get an excruciating, pus-engorged sore the size of a golf ball. And you won't get high. So don't fuck it up."

Jesus took a shuddering breath and wiped perspiration from his brow with the back of his clammy hand. He once more looked up at Lucifer with pleading eyes, but the latter only shook his head with cold resolve. "I've watched eight-year-old kids do it without even blinking, for fuck's sake. You can't tell me the Son of God can't do a simple shot of dope."

Blinking angrily, Jesus took another deep breath. The despair of the comedown was very quickly overcoming his anxiety, so with a calm that was jarring in its steadiness, he carefully slid the tip of the needle into a welcoming vein in the crook of his arm, wincing as he watched smoke-like plumes of scarlet billow up into the chamber of the syringe, mixing with the foreign concoction within. A quick glance at Lucifer, this time one of steadfast determination as opposed to childlike fear, yielded a mildly disconcerting glimpse of a smile that seemed somehow far more wicked than any he'd yet seen upon the devil's face. He paid it little mind, and returned his gaze to the needle in his arm.

*Fuck you, Dad*, he thought.

He pushed the stopper down.

"You're drooling."

Jesus looked around and blinked, searching for the source of the voice, which seemed so far away and garbled as if underwater. He was sitting at the bar, or *slouching*, if a more accurate term were to be applied, with his head lolling around atop his shoulders as if tethered there only barely and to a badly-oiled bearing. A filmy gray fog hung over his surroundings, and everything had a kind of nullified *nothing* sound to it, like barely-audible static on a television with the sound turned down. He had a stomach ache accompanied by slight nausea, and he vaguely remembered throwing up outside, but he didn't care; he was *high*, a word he'd never fully understood until his vein had drunk up that magical elixir and brought upon him this state of hazy transcendence.

High.

"You're drooling."

Jesus rubbed at his eyes, a slow and languid action that seemed to take far longer than it should have, and the blurry visage of Lucifer materialized on the barstool next to him. His lips were moving...but the words coming out didn't quite synch properly with his mouth, reminding Jesus of a poorly-dubbed *Godzilla* film.

"You're drooling," the devil was saying for what was either the third time or just a continued echo of the first. "Wipe your fucking mouth, dude, that's gross."

Jesus attempted to do just that, but his arms had trebled in weight since he'd raised them to rub his eyes just moment/s (singular? plural?) prior, so his left fell lifelessly into his lap and his right slid off the bar and came to just hang pathetic and disjointed at his side. He looked down at them, from one to the other and then back to the first, and something about all of this struck him as comical and he burst into a fit of wheezy giggles, until he could no longer support his head in its upright position so he let it fall to the bar, where he felt his cheek stick to something wet upon its surface so he realized that he *must* have been drooling, after all.

"How do you *feel*?" the fuzzy-shaped Japanese actor next to him was asking. "Is that coke crash starting to subside?"

Jesus snickered and said, "En uh zur-eds ut ee-o-ee-uh uz ad."

The Japanese man laughed and lit a cigarette. "Hiroshima

was *hilarious*," he said, leading Jesus to wonder if perhaps he *wasn't* a zipperhead as originally thought. With some effort he was able to peel his face from the bar and once again sit more or less upright, and the actor briefly came into focus and Jesus for a second remembered who he was and that he *wasn't* an actor, much less a zipperhead, and for that same second he remembered where they were and how he'd gotten here, all of it surging back in a dizzying rush that made him lightheaded and he almost threw up again (again? had he thrown up before?) but he choked it down and noticed that the burly men by the pool table were looking at him again, and not so nicely, so he mentioned this to Lucifer but Lucifer just frowned and told him he was being paranoid again, to just enjoy the high and stop worrying about stupid shit, so Jesus resolved to do exactly that even though he really couldn't say that he *was* worried so much as he was purely curious in a disinterested sort of way as to why the men might be interested in him, and he thought perhaps they wanted to fuck him, which now wasn't a terrible enough notion but he thought he would prefer it be the devil's dick inside of him as opposed to those men's sweaty steroid-shriveled disgraces.

"What's so funny?" the devil was asking, and Jesus started to ask what he meant until he realized he was laughing but couldn't recall why, and now that he thought about it, he couldn't even recall what he'd been thinking about a few seconds ago.  Male anatomy?  Steroids?  Toad the Wet Sprocket, or maybe J.M. Coetzee?  He kept trying to

*dolls everywhere…sprawled across the airport with their porcelain faces bashed in and their glass eyes rolling about on the tile…one of them crunches under a police officer's boot heel while stern-faced city servants stare at the scene, curled fake hair torn from rubber scalps of something that surely at one point in its life had it continued to exist would have been some little girl's best friend but perhaps this was not to be so and had it survived it would have gotten its own place and said FUCK THE WORLD and boots worn by boots are as classy as they come…you say you were talking to somebody about this yesterday; was she also a boot? did you know she was a boot? when you ask somebody something, perhaps when you tell them something, without doubt warrants response under circumstances that at the very least would be considered polite.*

Snapping fingers in his face…the long pale fingers of the devil…*snap snap snap*…"Billy-Bob, are you in there?  Earth to Billy-Bob.  Fuck, man, is there *anyone* in there?"

Jesus looked around blankly, as if groping along in the dark for a light switch that doesn't exist, blinking uselessly against a darkness that wasn't there and saying, "Um, I…who?  Who is…what?"

Disapproval…likely, Jesus assumed, directed at him, but from whom and for what he did not know, but

*sipping champagne in classy restaurants where the waiters all wear tuxedos and the customers sit around lethargic and fat, not in a manner we consider perhaps disgusting but just more reflective of their sense of comfort, many of whom clearly have EARNED that degree of comfort which they now possess because so many are HANDED comfort because of luck and little else but at the same time LUCK as a general concept could be referred to as...IRRELEVANT.*

The pool players were no longer playing pool and had come over to the bar to drink their beer, talking quietly among one another and stealing unsubtle glances at Jesus and Lucifer, but more so, Jesus thought, at *him*, and he thought vaguely about saying something to Lucifer again but then he realized no, the men are too close, they might overhear, and if they

*you can say things good or bad to people...f has p...which does not mean anything...perhaps a glitch perhaps an error perhaps...for service people? Just looking at that making this strictly a service elevator...is that correct? And by that I mean staying in this area.*

Jesus decided they were *definitely* talking about him, and whatever they were saying was not pleasant. Wait...was that Lucifer, talking to them now? Yes, it was, and *he* seemed to be talking about Jesus, too, but it certainly couldn't be anything bad, because he was his friend...his *lover*, and he wouldn't just

*howling court jesters and giggling faceless schoolgirls hopping scotch while Daddy pounds Becks at Beck's and the neighbors all talk among each other about each other because they are afraid to face themselves as well as what may become of them if they go searching for something and find it...because you can look and look and turn over every rock and look behind every tree and search every cave, batter down shanty doors with the sturdy stocks of your guns and shout and rustle about and throw things hither and thither, breaking that which appears to be of sentimental value and pocketing that which is of more MONETARY value to you and to US as a collective and shout WHERE ARE THEY and shout WHERE ARE YOU HIDING THEM and go crashing down the stairs and line up the cowering mice, ignoring their pleas, shooting them one by one and keeping the cheese from their traps because it was always entitled to you anyway.*

Talking *to* him now, or *at* him, rather, loudly and angrily, coating Jesus' face with spittle and bombarding his nostrils with the proximity of their alcohol-reeking breath, and Jesus tried to listen to what they were saying at him but they were too loud and every time he tried to strain himself to hear he kept remembering that he just didn't give a shit, so

*pink clouds and slinking purple cats on playgrounds under the earth, whispering to each other gently and caressing their ears with their twitching tails and speaking of things only that can be known by those among them, to never be divulged to anyone lest it ruin everyone...to move is TOO MUCH, to interact perhaps equally so, but to SIT and SINK in the dark in COMFORT and in BLISS is the ESSENTIAL ANSWER to the question nagging at everyone's mind...even the ones who think they've figured it out.*

They dragged him across the floor, kicking and beating

him, but there was no pain.  He looked dazedly about for the devil but saw him nowhere, so he could only wonder with passing disinterest why this

*your sticky corrosive tar is bubbling within my blackening heart, causing it to wither and fester like a gangrenous leprosy sore…you are my bloodshot eyes and I am your pinprick pupil…you are my tracks…my bleeding, reddened nose…my shivering night sweats.*

He was shoved out into the parking lot and beaten some more, the men cheering gaily as they drank their beer and pelted him with blows he thought were quite undeserved, but then again, what did he know?  It was all very strange, but everything was so far away that he just couldn't be bothered to give a damn, not even when they tossed him into the bed of a pickup truck and struck him over the head with a

*scholarly turtles in professor settings, peering over the rims of their spectacles at their students, looking out over the blank faces of the fish while everyone around me is drunk, happily unaware of their unhappiness…I can see for miles past the water over to endless lands that begin nowhere and have no shore…there's that heavy numbness…that slurred everything…that unspeakable, undeniable EVERYTHING…and we can't run from or to it, it is only there…and we can see everything because we can see nothing…scratch that…we can see nothing because we can see everything.*

* * *

Jesus' head throbbed upon waking. His eyes opened to a darkness only slightly less than the one from which he'd awoken, and the air was damp and musty. His stomach hurt and his joints ached.

He tried to remember where he'd last been, but the only image he could conjure up was Lucifer's grinning face. When he attempted to cry out for help, he found his throat to be too dry and sore to muster up anything louder than a raspy whisper.

"Hey, look, I think he's waking up."

The voice sounded gruff and throaty, and a little put-on, as though a portion of its masculine depth was exaggerated.

"Shit, I think you're right," came another voice of similar timbre but without as much showy machismo. "So what are we gonna do with him?"

Something was yanked off Jesus' head and he could suddenly see again; he was lying in the grass beneath a cloudy night sky, looking up at one of the burly men from the bar, who was glaring down at him and holding a burlap sack, which Jesus now realized was what had been upon his head.

"I texted Father Benway about twenty minutes ago," said the one with the sack. "He should be here any minute. He sounded excited."

Jesus tried to sit up, but his body hurt too much for him to move, and his hands and feet were bound with thick plastic zipties. "Where am I?" he asked groggily. "Who are you? What's going on?" About fifteen feet away, the other two members of the foursome were digging a hole that was already up to their waists, leading Jesus to wonder how long he'd been out. He strained his eyes to look around, and ascertained that they were in a wide clearing surrounded by dense, dark forest.

"This is where you're gonna die," said the overly gruff one, who sat chomping a cigar on a stump a few yards to the sack-bearers left.

"What do you think, Ted...should we have some fun with him?" asked the other one. He grinned down at Jesus, his smile yellow and stained with tobacco juice.

Ted, the cigar-smoker, said, "Easy there, Georgie...we need to wait for Benway. We shouldn't do anything without him givin us the go-ahead, first. If he wants him for tomorrow's mass, he probably won't want us roughin him up any more than we already have."

"How's he gonna know the difference?" said Georgie, twisting the sack in his hands and leering greedily at Jesus, who swallowed nervously. His head was still extremely fuzzy and he was having trouble keeping up with all of this, but he at least knew that he was in trouble.

"Just hold your horses," said Ted, picking up a bottle of Bud Light from the grass and taking a huge swig. "Like you said, he'll be here any minute." He looked over his shoulder at the hole-diggers and called, "How's that hole comin along, boys?"

One of them shouted back, "It would come along a lot faster if you two fucks would come over and help!"

Ted chuckled and puffed on his cigar.

Jesus heard footsteps approaching through the brush, snapping twigs and crunching leaves, and a flashlight beam cut into the dark like a huge white knife. A short old man emerged from the edge of the forest and came to stand beside Georgie. He wore all black, save for the white clerical band at his collar. Brushing nettles and leaves from his shirt, he glared down at Jesus and said, "So," he said, "this is the heretic."

"Yes, Father," said Georgie, giving Jesus a swift kick to the ribs. "Rich fellow we met at the Bad Seed said he happened across him in an alley, hollerin and rantin about how he's 'the son of God' and whatnot. Apparently he followed him to the bar, and when the rich guy tried to ditch him out back, this loony fucktard shot up some dope and then came right back in. So we told the dude that we'd find a safe place for his crazy friend."

*Huh?* Jesus thought in his delirium. *No. No. What? No, Lucifer cares about me, he'd never do that to me.*

"At first we thought we'd take him out here and kill him and bury him," said Ted, coming over to stand by Georgie and the priest, "but then we decided to call you out here to take a look at him and see if you wanted to use him as the sacrifice at tomorrow's mass. We know it's short notice, though, so if you've already got someone lined up, we've got that hole there and we'll be more than happy to take care of him for you."

The priest stroked his chin, scrutinizing Jesus. "I do indeed have a sacrifice prepared for tomorrow's mass," he said, "and under different circumstances I'd take this man off your hands and keep him for next week. But…this is a *special* kind of heretic. He…"

"I am…the son of…God," Jesus croaked. "I am your lord…and savior."

Georgie kicked him again, harder, and spat on his face.

"As I was saying," said Benway, "this wretched creature is so low that he doesn't even *deserve* a Catholic sacrifice. Heretics and naysayers are one thing, but *this*…a man who claims to be *Jesus Christ Himself*…no, I wouldn't desecrate the holy ground of our church with his foul presence. You may do to him as you please."

*God…Daddy…please,* Jesus prayed silently. *I don't know what's going on, but if you truly love me, you will save me from this. Strike down these men. Save me, please, please, save me.*

The two gravediggers came over, wiping sweat from their faces with the cuffs of their sleeves. One of them clapped the priest on the back and said, "Good to see you, Father. How's my boy been treatin ya?"

"Very nicely, thank you," answered the priest. "He gives

the best blowjobs in Mudhoney County, and that's no small feat; I've gotten *a lot* of blowjobs from *a lot* of boys."

"He fuckin better," said the gravedigger, nodding appreciatively. "I made him practice on me for years before I made him become an altar boy and turned him over to you. His own mother ain't got shit on those juicy young lips. But if you wasn't satisfied with him, I'd beat him to kingdom fuckin come, I swear it to Jesus." He looked down at Christ and said, "The *real* Jesus, anyhow."

"No need for beatings," said Benway. "He's doing just fine. Tight little asshole, he's got, too."

"I'm glad to hear that. I was worried it'd be stretched out from all the times I done caught his brother fuckin him in the shed."

"You'd be surprised just how resilient are the assholes of young boys."

"Speaking of assholes," said Georgie, "how's about we plug this here one's up with the cocks of righteousness?"

There were murmurings of enthusiastic agreement.

They all took turns with him, all four of the big men from the bar, while the priest stood off to the side, smoking cigarettes and watching passively.

Georgie kicked Jesus over on his stomach and cut his trousers off with a rusty box cutter, the dull-ish blade painfully grazing his skin as it tore through fabric and thread. Jesus was biting down hard on his lip but couldn't keep from whimpering.

When he entered Jesus, it at first felt pleasant, the hard warm obstruction stimulating nerve endings as it penetrated deep into his anal cavity, and Jesus moaned softly as he hearkened back to those precious moments with Lucifer in the strip club bathroom. His cock stiffened.

But then it started to feel different.

Then it started to *hurt*. His cock withered.

"God, Father, save me!" Jesus cried when Ted took over once Georgie was done. "Lucifer, where art thou? Why have you forsaken me?"

One of the other men said disgustedly, "Hear that shit, boys? Fucker's got a hardon for Satan, too."

*If only they knew*, Jesus thought.

"He is a heretic of the most poisonous breed," came the old, strained voice of the priest. "He must be destroyed, and utterly."

The third man slashed as Jesus' back with something sharp, maybe the other one's box cutter, as he fucked him and laughed heartily. The fourth broke a beer bottle over his head when he was done, and then plunged the jagged remains into his side and dragged it upward, scraping his ribs. Blood fed the grass and pooled in the curled basins of dead leaves.

They shoved him over on his back and kicked him and beat him with sticks. One of them kept stomping on his face with a heavy, steel-toed boot. He felt his jaw break a few times and he had to keep swallowing sharp pieces of dislodged teeth to prevent himself from choking on them. They sliced up his throat on the way down.

His eyes were bleeding. One of them rolled loosely in its socket. His nose was busted so badly that it bent at such an angle so the tip rested against his cheek. The blows to his stomach and chest caused him to puke blood and he had to turn his head to the side to cough out thick mouthfuls of it. The boot came down on the side of his head and as part of his face caved in he wondered vaguely how he was still conscious.

Somehow, though, much of the pain was far away…there, but distant. He attributed this to the heroin. Once they started kicking at his groin, however, the pain became very real. He felt his testicles burst, tried to scream but only spurted out a dark concoction of blood and bile and teeth.

One of them procured a long knife that beamed sinister in the starlight, and he knelt down so he could saw savagely into Jesus' abdomen. The others crowded around and started pulling out the pink ropes of his intestines. The priest was laughing haggardly.

When they grew tired of playing with his innards, one of them seized him by his long hair and began dragging him towards the hole. His guts trailed after him like weary afterthoughts.

Lying there in the hole, he couldn't feel the gasoline being poured onto him, but he could smell it as the fumes pervaded his mostly-exposed sinuses. He looked up at the men above him with his remaining good eye, and for a moment saw not five men but six...the priest, the four from the bar, and *the devil*. The latter stood grinning wildly, there but not, almost shimmering with faint translucence. But then he was gone, and the priest said, "Baptism by fire, motherfucker," and then he took a final drag from his smoldering cigarette before casting it casually into the hole.

Jesus awakened sharply on a velvet couch inside a vast, plush hotel lobby. The pain was gone, and Lucifer was back, sitting in an armchair across from him with a cigarette between his fingers and a smile on his face.

"Rise and shine, kiddo," Lucifer said. And then, "I've been waiting a very, very long time for this."

Jesus rubbed at his eyes. "Waiting for *what*?" he asked, anger creeping through the tired grogginess in his voice. "What the *fuck*, man? Did you sell me out to those guys? Did you know they would do those things to me? Did you let them *kill* me? Am I *dead*?"

"No one is ever *really* dead," said the devil, "and

especially not you. But to the rest of your questions, yes."

Jesus' bottom lip trembled and his eyes filled with tears. "But...why? Why would you betray me like that?"

With mocking sarcasm, Lucifer said, "Oh *heavens*, who*ever* would have thought that the devil was capable of *deceit?* Certainly the Prince of Lies would never *actually* lie, right?"

Leaning forward and massaging his temples, Jesus said, "So, wait...all those things you told me...about my dad, about the world, about *you*...none of that was true?"

"Oh, no, *that* was all true. In fact, come to think of it, I never *outright* lied to you about *anything*. My only *sin*, here, if you will, was misleading you to think that I actually give even *half* of a fuck about you. I told you the truth about everything else, but it wasn't because I had any real concern for *you*."

"Then...why? Why enlighten me to all these terrible truths?"

Smiling wider and hitting his cigarette, the devil answered, "Because I wanted to win the bet. And what better way to defeat God than to give you the very thing that He has hidden from you all your life? That being, of course, *knowledge*. The most dangerous thing in the universe. It has an incredible capacity to destroy and corrupt, and it succeeded just as grandly this time as it has all the others."

"I thought...you and I...we *had* something. We...*we made*

*love."*

Lucifer blinked, was silent, and then burst into cruel laughter. *"Made love?"* he repeated in disbelief. "Are you out of your fucking *head*, Christ? Fuck, man, I sodomized you because it was a perfect *fuck you* to your old man. I'd really already won the bet, but by that point I was just kind of rubbing it in, so to speak. I mean, when God created you, the *last* thing He had planned was for you to end up on your knees sucking the devil's dick and then getting rammed up the ass with it. I'm *never* going to let Him live that one down."

Jesus was weeping silently by now. "So," he said, "you never felt *anything* for me? You never felt that…connection?"

Raising his eyebrows, Lucifer said, "In the name of your father, kid, have you lost your *goddamn* mind? *Listen* to yourself. I'm the fuckin *devil*. Did you *really* think I'd gone all soft and mushy inside just because I plugged you in a strip club bathroom? Look, I'll be square with you. Beelzebub and I had a side-bet going on. He wagered that, no matter what happened, I wouldn't be able to get you to suck my dick. And you see, my poor man, I don't like to lose."

Jesus flushed with shameful embarrassment. "A farce," he said. "It was all a farce. All of it. Ever since the very beginning."

"Shit, son, ain't *that* the truth. Don't take it so hard. Oh, wait, I guess you kinda already did, huh?" He sniggered as

Jesus wept harder. "Too soon? Poor taste? Did I hurt your feelings, O Holy One?"

Jesus wiped his eyes and said, "When did you turn so mean?"

The devil shrugged. "When did you turn into such a bitch? The answer to both questions is the same, so figure it out. Now, aren't you curious as to why you're here, and not up in Heaven playing patty-cake with cherubs?"

Jesus nodded, even though the cherubs preferred "Go Fish" to patty-cake. He didn't think that particular detail was worth mentioning.

"Well," said Lucifer, standing up, "come see for yourself." He held out his hand to Jesus, and Jesus took it.

The ballroom was occupied by an excitedly chattering welcoming party, most of them drinking pink champagne. There were knives and hatchets and blunt weapons on many of the tables. When Jesus and the devil entered, the group grew quiet.

"You don't know these folks," Lucifer said to Jesus, "because you have ignored all of them. They know you, though. They know you very well, and they aren't tremendously fond of you."

"Why?" Jesus asked, his voice innocent and confused. "I never did anything to anyone."

One of the men stepped forward and said, "More like, you never did anything *for* anyone. You let the world run riot with excess." His eyes were tired and he was holding the hand of a small child. The boy's pants were soaked. "Worthless leaders, careless managers...a hierarchy of ignorance that thrives on the copious abundance of *things*, while the lowly struggle and suffer."

A woman emerged, dressed in a white lab coat, and said, "And what about me? I was so miserable, all the time. No one could help me...not my fiance, not my lovers, not my brother, and certainly not *you*. I was always covered in grime and it wouldn't stay off no matter how many showers I took."

Jesus again opened his mouth to speak, but before he could, another man stepped forward and said, "The buzzing in my head never stopped. Fucking buzzing. You could have made it go away, I think. My parents, they said you had the power to do anything, but you didn't take away my buzzing. And then I came here. This place made it go away. Because of Lucifer and his kindness."

A man with a cheese grater in his hand said, "I had to destroy myself just to be free. You never gave me freedom. You could have, but you didn't."

Another man, this one timid and skittish-looking and

adorned in clothes covered in blood, said, "Yeah, and where the fuck were you when that little pissant kid took my wife from me? You could have struck him dead, but I had to take matters into my own hands. And even that didn't help. You could have given me something, *anything* to make life worth living, but even killing the asshole wasn't enough to stop *my* sickness. It seems to me like a lot of us are, or *were*, at least, pretty fucking sick in one way or another. And you...what did you do?"

Two women pushed through the crowd to stand at the front. One was shockingly beautiful, the other bloated and haggard and sickly. They both held entire bottles of champagne. "My Jane, my Crazy Jane, she was there for me when you weren't," said the gross one. "Fuck you. *Fuck...you.* And I bet you can't eat pussy nearly as well as she does, you pompous piece of shit."

"Don't worry," the other woman said to Jesus. "*I* took care of her. It appears that another common thread here is that most of us got help from someone or something else while you sat in your clouds and ignored us all."

A man with a crew cut and military fatigues said, "I saw some things that no loving God would ever have allowed. I had to do things that..." He trailed off, looking down at his boots. "I was just following orders," he said quietly.

The next man to speak was tall and thin and gray-haired, and he held a cup of steaming coffee in his hand. He wasn't wearing shoes. "I prayed, you know," he said. "Never helped. I just got worse and drank more. Fuck, I had to crash on some planet out of a Bradbury novel in order to get fixed. The things there cured me, but you weren't among them."

"Listen," Jesus said loudly. "I'm *busy*, okay? I run the bingo club four nights a week, and the cherubs need to hear their stories. Plus, my dad gives me all sorts of chores. I have to do my own laundry. I walk Shiloh *and* Winn Dixie. Sometimes I even have to make my own *dinner*, and once, I had to scrub a *toilet*. I just don't have *time* to get to everyone's prayers." He looked at the devil and said, "Why am I here? Why are *they* here? What's going on?"

Grinning that grin of his, Lucifer said, "I won the bet, remember? And the stakes were, if I won, I got to make you a permanent resident of the Hotel Empyrean. Unfortunately for *you*, though, you're not a Platinum Member like the others, here. You see, these folks have been requesting your presence for a very long time. I promise to fulfill all of my prized residents' desires, but bringing *you* here has been the one thing on which I just couldn't deliver. I pride myself on my hospitality, though, and I assured them that one day they would have their chance to do to you as they please."

Jesus took a step back on his Jell-O legs. "And…um…what do they want to do to me, exactly?"

The devil shrugged. "I don't know, man. Ask them."

The angry sinners, smiling and relishing in all of their newfound privilege that they'd been denied all their lives, started putting down their drinks and picking up the various weapons.

"You can't die, here," Lucifer said. "But you can feel pain."

The armed men and women were advancing, even the child, brandishing their weapons in hands shaking with anticipation and excitement.

"They'll be busy with you for a long time, I suspect," the devil continued. "And once they decide to take a break, I'm quite sure I'll have more residents who'd like to take a turn."

Jesus turned to flee, but the door that had been there moments ago had been replaced by an endless wall made of white bricks. He looked over his shoulder at the approaching attackers, and then he collapsed onto the floor, his legs no longer able to withstand the all-consuming fear that had seized his body.

The devil had vanished, but his disembodied voice thundered from somewhere in the darkness and said, "That's it, kiddo. Make yourself comfortable. You're in this for the long haul. You can check out anytime you like, but you can never leave."

Jesus would go on to scream forever, but God did not listen.

God listens to no one.

Printed in Great Britain
by Amazon